Paid For Death

Niles Rader

CENTAUR BOOKS
Chicago

Paid For Death
Niles Rader

Centaur Books by Niles Rader

Rice Brothers Mysteries:
Betrayed By Greed
Death by Deceit
Death Does Not Wait
Death Was Inevitable
Dumb Luck Pays Off
The Root of Evil

Other Mysteries:
A Sister's Revenge
Lie To Love
Live Smart or Die Dumb
Paid for Death
Paid for Death The Return
Retribution Vengeance is Mine

Published by CENTAUR BOOKS
CentaurBooks.com

CENTAUR BOOKS
Chicago

imprint of Joshua Tree Publishing
JoshuaTreePublishing.com
• Chicago •

13-Digit ISBN: 978-0-9710954-8-9
First Printing 2005 Second Printing 2015

Chapter 1

Jessie left Camp Perry in Virginia and drove straight through to St. Louis, Missouri. He made arrangements for his lodging and drove to the Appollo Nursing Home where his father had been for the past three months. He went in to meet with Dr. Kennis and talk to him about his father. They walked to a lounge where Dr. Kennis poured them both a cup of coffee and sat down at one of the tables.

"I wish I could give you some encouraging news about your father's condition, but I have to be honest with you," Dr. Kennis said. "Last week his organs started shutting down, and his heart and lungs are working at about twenty five percent. I've called in another doctor for his opinion, and we both agree that he could go at anytime. Please don't feel bad if he doesn't recognize you; he just doesn't seem to be aware of anything at this point."

"Thanks Doc for all you've done. I'll be staying at Howard Johnson's so I can be close to him. Right now, I think I'll go in and sit with him for awhile and thanks again. Here's my cell number so please call me if anything should change when I'm not here with him." With that, Jessie left the lounge and went to his father's room.

Jessie was shocked at the sight of his father lying in the bed. He was but a skeleton of the man he used to be. He had IVs in both arms, and his face was hidden behind an oxygen mask. If it weren't for the steady beep of the heart monitor, you would have thought him dead. Jessie pulled a chair close to the bed and held his father's hand that was cold because of the limited blood supply. He talked to his dad, sharing memories of past times and not knowing if his words were heard or understood.

"Dad, I'm sorry for not being here when Mom died but later today, I'm going to the cemetery to visit at her gravesite. I'm on furlough for awhile so I'll be here often to spend time with you, but because I drove all night, I'm pretty tired so I'm going to leave and get some rest. I'll be back tomorrow to spend more time with you." Jessie leaned down and kissed his father's forehead. "Bye for now Dad."

Jessie passed the nurse's station and saw the doctor sitting there. "Doc, you were right, he doesn't look good."

"No, he doesn't," the doctor said, "but there's something I have to give you following his imminent passing. Your mother and dad gave me a small fireproof box to give to you, but only when both are deceased."

"What's in the box?" Jessie asked.

"They said some stocks and a letter from both of them." The doctor continued, "They made me swear to them that you only get it when they're both gone."

"Then you need to keep your promise," Jessie said, "and looking at my dad, it won't be long. I'll be back tomorrow but right now I'm going to my motel and get some rest. I'll see you tomorrow."

Jessie drove back to the motel and after a shower and shave, went to the restaurant off the motel lobby. He ate light, as he was deep in thought and sorry that the inevitable passing of his father could not be altered. After a somewhat fitful night's rest, he rose, took a quick shower, shaved, and had a light breakfast.

Jessie drove to the cemetery, following the directions his dad had given him before he became ill. He went directly to the family plot that had been acquired a few years earlier. He looked at the large headstone on his mother's grave bearing only her name on the left side, Carol Ruben. He noticed that no date of birth or death was printed there and made a mental note to make the arrangements to have the headstone completed.

He knelt down beside the grave and said, "Well Mom, I finally got here. I hope you can forgive me for being gone so much over the last few years and for not being here when you passed away. I went by to see Dad and as I sit here with you, I know that it won't be long before you'll be together again very soon."

Jessie was overwhelmed by the total sadness of it all; and although it was necessary to wipe away the tears that flowed uncontrollably, he continued talking. He told her about the new job he was considering and said, "Even if I have to leave before Dad does, I'll be back for his funeral."

"Mom, I miss you and Dad so much, but I'll come back here to visit every chance I get. Maybe Dad will recognize me today, but if not, perhaps you'll tell him I was here talking with you."

The time Jessie spent at his mother's gravesite seemed to stand still as all the emotions and memories from all the years gone by poured out. Jessie finally said goodbye to his mother, promising to return again soon, then left the cemetery to return to the nursing home and his dying father.

Chapter 2

Jessie met with the doctor and asked him if there was any change in his dad's condition. The doctor told him that the breathing was becoming more labored, his kidneys were beginning to fail, and although life supports were available should he want them used, the doctor said, "My guess for his time remaining is less than a week with his organs shutting down as they are. Of course, no one knows the actual time, only the One above."

"That's so true," Jessie said, "but Dad signed a paper that no life supports are to be used. He never wanted to be kept alive and just lay there. My parents believed that dying was a time for celebration because they would be together again."

"A long time ago I asked Pop about heaven and hell. His answer was that it is better to be prepared and find out there is none, than not be prepared and find out there is."

With that said, Jessie told the doctor he wanted to spend time with his dad. As he entered his father's room, he could tell by the steady beep, beep of the heart monitor that his father's heart was slowing down, as was his breathing

"Hello Pop," Jessie said, "I thought you might like to know that I went to visit mom this morning and I noticed that there's no dates on the headstone. I'll talk to the funeral director and get the appropriate dates engraved on her marker.

"Dad, I hate to see you go, but I know you want to see Mom—and I know she's looking forward to seeing you too. I'm sorry we haven't been able to talk, but I believe you hear me so I'll tell you now: I love you both so much and want to thank you for being such good parents to a guy that was sometimes a little hard to handle. God willing, I'll see you both again."

Jessie fell silent for the next couple hours just holding his father's hand and watching and hearing the heart monitor. He couldn't believe the depth of the sadness he felt, and again, his mind wandered to days gone by and times past.

Jessie was brought out of his reverie when the door opened and Doctor Kennis came in with another doctor. "Jessie, this is Dr. Harris, and he's here to examine your dad. Why don't you go to the waiting room for a few minutes, and he'll come out and talk with you."

Jessie complied with the doctor's request and went to the waiting room, got a soft drink from the vending machine, and waited for the news he was certain would not be good. He didn't have long to wait and knew from the expression on the doctor's faces that the news they were about to give him was what he had expected.

"Mr. Ruben, I was here almost a week ago for the same tests," Dr. Harris began the conversation. "I told Dr. Kennis then, that without life support, maybe your Dad had three weeks. Now, and I'm sorry to tell you this, but I believe we are down to a matter of hours. Any life support given now would only delay the end and could not improve his condition."

"My father has a living will so that's already been settled," Jessie said. "No life supports. What will happen if we turn off the oxygen?"

Dr. Kennis said, "We can't say for sure except for now, it's helping him breathe."

"I'd like to spend some time with him," Jessie said, "and tell him what we're going to do. Then I'd like to have the oxygen turned off. Once that's done, we'll let nature take its course."

"Please go in Mr. Ruben," Dr. Kennis said. "We'll come in when you call us."

Once again, Jessie sat in the chair beside his father's bed, picked up the cool and seemingly lifeless hand, and explained what they were planning to do.

"Dad, if you're ready to leave, please tell Mom what we've talked about. But in any case, I'll stay here with you as long as you want to stay with me."

Jessie stood up, leaned over and kissed his father's forehead. "I love you Dad." With that, he called the doctors into his father's room. Once Dr. Kennis turned off the oxygen, Jessie watched the heart monitor begin to slow down and within a minute, the breathing stopped—his father was gone. With tears in his eyes, Jessie once more leaned down to kiss his father's forehead and said, "Go to God and to Mom."

Jessie left the room, feeling a terrible sadness and ache in his heart. He knew that the hospital had the number for the funeral parlor and told the nurse he'd be back in the morning to see the doctor.

With his head down and a heavy heart, he left the hospital to return to his hotel.

Chapter 3

Jessie was sure he would not get much sleep this night so he stopped at a liquor store and bought a bottle of booze and a 6-pack of beer. Once he was back in his room, he showered and then watched TV. He downed a couple shots followed by beer chasers and to his surprise, found he was finally able to relax like when a hard day's work is over. Still, there was deep sadness at his father's passing but also a peaceful feeling that the suffering was over and now he was with Mom. After drinking a few more suds, Jessie laid back on the couch. The next thing he knew, it was morning.

While eating breakfast, Jessie tried to plan his day. First he would go see the doctor, then the funeral director about the headstone to add his father's name with dates of birth and death and complete the dates on his mother's headstone. Once the funeral was over, there was no reason to hang around so he would call the office and let them know he would be returning for work earlier than originally planned.

Jessie finished his breakfast and was soon seated across the desk from the doctor. The doctor reached into the desk drawer and handed Jessie a small, fireproof box. "I'm sorry to have to give this to you under these circumstances, Mr. Ruben, but these were the wishes of your parents."

Jessie thanked him for the box and also for taking such good care of his parents.

"I won't open this until I get back to my room," Jessie said. "From here, I'm going to the funeral parlor to arrange for dad's burial. After the funeral, I have to leave so I'll say goodbye now and thanks again for all you did for my folks."

Jessie drove to the funeral home and met with the funeral director. He expressed his desires regarding the headstones and the plans for the funeral. It was decided that the service would be held Wednesday at 9 a.m.

"Is there anything else I should do?" Jessie asked.

"No, Mr. Ruben," the funeral director said. "All the details for the funeral were completed by your folks, including the casket and clothes they were to be buried in because they weren't sure you could be home to make all the arrangements."

"That's true," Jessie said. "I was overseas when Mom died and just got back a couple weeks ago. I've taken a month off to be here, but I have to get back soon as I have a new job waiting for me. Wednesday for the funeral works out fine for me. I'm staying at the Howard Johnson's room 31 so please call me if there's any change in plans. In the meantime, I'll try to contact some people regarding dad's funeral."

Jessie left the funeral home and returned to his room. The more he thought about who to call, the more he realized he knew very little about what went on in the past year. His parents had moved to this area shortly before his mother passed away. He had no idea who to call to advise of his father's funeral. At least it would be in the newspaper so people would read about it and attend if they wanted to.

Jessie decided the time had come to find out what information his parents had left for him so he grabbed a beer and sat down on the sofa to open the fireproof box. He flipped on the TV, opened the box, and saw that inside were a few stock certificates. Under them was an envelope addressed to "Our son Jessie."

Removing the papers from the envelope, he began to read the letter:

To Our Dear Son Jessie,

This is the hardest letter we've ever had to write, and we're so sorry that we didn't tell you in person.

Many years ago, Dad was a member of the Gulardi Family. When the gang wars started, most of the Family split apart. Your father and I got away, along with two suitcases full of money and a baby entrusted to us by his mother. She later died, as did her husband. With everyone else dead that we knew of, we adopted the baby and never told him of his adoption.

Remember Jessie, how fair-skinned we were? What about your size compared to your dad and me? At 6'1" and 235 lbs., you make two of your adopted dad. Your real father was a large man, and your mother was beautiful. We changed your name to Jessie Ruben, but your real name was Raymond Gulardi. The last promise we made to your mother was to keep you safe and love you as our own.

As you know, we didn't have any other children so all our love was only for you.

As you look through this box, you'll see that the stocks are in your name so you can retire whenever you want as their value is worth a fortune.

We hope you can forgive us for not telling you sooner. May you always remember how much we have loved you. Now we'll say our last goodbye. Please take care of yourself. Love Forever, Mom and Dad.

P.S. You were born in Philly, PA twenty years ago.

Jessie read the letter again and again with tears in his eyes. Finally he folded the letter and slid it back into the envelope. Next he took the stocks and looked through them but had no idea as to their value. It didn't matter because he made a good living and had no one to take care of. He decided that when he returned to Virginia, he'd put them in a safety deposit box at the bank.

That night as Jessie replayed the events of the day, all he could think about was whether or not any of his real relatives were still alive. Virginia was not far from New Jersey so maybe he could pull a few strings and find out. After all, he had a name and a date so perhaps he could do some investigation and see what could be turned up.

Gulardi from Philly, twenty-three years ago. Maybe he could find out where his real parents were buried. Working for the government had some advantages that could open doors normally closed to other people. Who knew, maybe some relative could be found. At this point in time, he realized that there was nothing he could do except to relax tomorrow and go to his father's funeral on Wednesday.

* * * * *

Jessie was up early on the day of his father's funeral. Once he was dressed, he stopped by the restaurant for a quick breakfast. When he finished, he drove to the funeral home and went to sit close to his father's body.

"Well Dad," Jessie said, "I read the letter and was quite surprised at everything you and Mom told me about. I had wondered about the difference in our skin color, but nothing could ever change how I feel about you both. No one could have had a better childhood or have been more loved than me. Now I understand why we didn't stay in one place very long and somehow I wondered about the Ruben name.

Was that your real name or did you take it before or when you adopted me? Really, it doesn't matter now as the government accepted me into the service. After I leave here, I'll see if any relatives are still in the Philly area. With a name like Gulardi, they shouldn't be too hard too find.

Jessie looked at his watch and realized it was time to start the funeral. The funeral director asked him about going to the gravesite to hold the final rites. Jessie agreed so they proceeded to the gravesite. As the dirt was being put on the coffin, Jessie gave the director his address and asked him to send a picture of his parent's grave once the headstones had been completed. With everything now finished, Jessie returned to his motel to check out.

Chapter 4

Jessie decided he'd drive tonight until he got tired and then find a room for the night. Around 9:00 p.m., he pulled into a motel knowing that by tomorrow evening, he would be back at the base in Virginia. Up at dawn, he drove most of the way to Camp Perry, a little known, somewhat secured, training base where even the people who live in that area didn't know what goes on there. Only the people who are stationed or work there have a clue; even then, some of the civilians were still in the dark as to training programs and techniques.

He arrived late in the afternoon and stayed at a motel in Williamsburg, Virginia. The next morning he drove to the camp to see what was in store for him. At the reception desk he introduced himself and asked whom he should talk to.

"Mr. Ruben," the receptionist said, "you're to see Mr. Jacobe. I'll inform him that you're here."

Jessie heard her say, "Yes sir, I'll send him right down."

"Mr. Ruben, Mr. Jacobe will see you now. His office is the last door down at the end of the hall." Jessie thanked her and walked down the hall.

Just as he was about to knock, the door suddenly opened, and Mr. Jacobe invited him in. Jessie introduced himself.

"Please call me Frank," Mr. Jacobe said, "as we don't have to be formal here. If you don't mind, I'll use your first name also."

"I don't mind, and in fact, I prefer it that way," Jessie agreed.

"Good, have a seat and we'll get started on what your new job entails. Would you care for some coffee?"

"Thank you sir, that sounds great."

"Jessie," he said, "You don't have to say Sir anymore because you're no longer in the service."

"I know," Jessie said, "but it's a hard habit to break."

"Jessie, every once in awhile we have someone recommended to us by people who know of a talent we can use. These people are invited in to talk to us, and you have been recommended. You have an understanding of two languages; and although you aren't that fluent in one, at least you can understand what's being said. Your skin is darker than most Caucasians so you could pass for some other race. With your survival training and other talents, you are an ideal candidate for the organization. We're attached to a couple branches of the Government, which are Treasury, Alcohol and Tobacco. Our job is usually that of infiltrating gangs and dealing with some pretty bad people. Most of the time you'd be on your own so danger is prevalent.

"Before I continue, the choice is up to you, but once you agree to join the group, the only time you can quit is when the job is finished—or we pull you out for your own safety. Each job you agree to do must be completed. However, once a job is done, you can stop working for us whenever you choose."

"Before we go any further," Jessie interrupted, "I have a couple questions I need to have answered before I answer you. How far can I go in order to stay alive?"

"We know nothing unless you tell us," Mr. Jacobe said. You are your own boss. We wait for word from you on your progress. We give you a phone number to call when you're ready to make contact or need something, but otherwise we don't know you. One more thing, when you accept, we give you all the information we have on your target. Do you have any more questions?"

"No, not right now," Jessie said, "but I may, once I get started. I do have a favor to ask though. Years ago there was a family named Gulardi from the East Coast, around Philly. I've been told that most of them were killed, but could you find out if there are any members of the family still alive?"

"Does this mean you have accepted the job?" Mr. Jacobe asked.

"Yes, I will accept the job," Jessie said, "if what you said is true that I can quit after the first one if I want."

"We hope you won't quit," Mr. Jacobe replied, "but we give all our people the same guarantee. Be here tomorrow morning at

7a.m. We'll have a film set up to show you your job and the people involved."

"That leads me to my next question," Jessie said, "How many people will know what I'm working on?"

"Only the Director, your contact, and me," Mr. Jacobe said, "and that's to ensure there aren't any leaks."

"Good," Jessie said, "so on that note I'll say goodbye and see you tomorrow."

It was still early so Jessie decided to head to the bank to rent a safety deposit box for the metal box containing the stocks and information that had come in the envelope, including the letter from his folks. Once all the personal information was safely locked away, he decided that once he had dinner, he'd rent a motel room.

He was still pretty wired from all the events from the last few days but after calling for a 6am wake-up call, he just kicked back to relax for awhile. Jessie fell into a deep sleep and was surprised that the wake-up call came so soon because it seemed to him that he had just laid down. Once up, he quickly shaved and showered, left the motel, and picked up a coffee on his way to the meeting.

Chapter 5

When Jessie arrived, the receptionist was expecting him and told him to go back to the same room he had been in the prior day. When he opened the door, there were two people waiting for him.

"Good morning Jessie," Mr. Jacobe said, "I hope you had a good night's sleep. I'd like you to meet Gene Howard. He's your phone contact and has some excellent input on this case, as he's been involved for over a year. Gene's knowledge of the area and who's who will give you a great start. Gene, why don't you give Jessie a little history of the situation and some idea of who and what he'll have to look out for."

"OK, I can do that," Gene said. "First Jessie, there are three groups that have somehow joined together to control all of Camden, New Jersey, about half of Philly and they're working on Newark. They're involved in gambling, prostitution, dope and now we hear gun running as well. Whatever else they're into, we're not sure yet. That's where you come in. We want you to infiltrate this gang and find out who's the real boss behind it all. We believe that one good man could destroy them from the inside—that's you. Now, let me show you some of the hangouts and those involved in this little group."

As the video was playing, Gene explained the locations and the people involved. "It appears that these four guys are some of the hirelings, and the next ones are involved when they have a meeting; but how, we don't know."

When the tape finished, Gene gave Jessie a stack of pictures of some of the men, along with their names written on them. "These you can study, remember each one, and then destroy them. Do you have any questions?"

"You said one good man could destroy them from the inside," Jessie said, "Does that mean *whatever it takes?* Am I reading this correctly?"

"Yes you are the best way to kill a snake is to cut off the head by whatever means you can. The difference between this and some of the other jobs you've handled is that dealers in drugs and guns don't care who they hurt or kill; all they care about is the money. We feel that with your training, knowledge of two languages and your upbringing, your judgment will not be clouded but when needed, there won't be any hesitation on your part to do what has to be done. Here's a phone number that's good any time of the day or night. Memorize it and destroy the card. We'll set up a bank account for you to use for whatever you need, along with this credit card and a couple thousand in cash. When you leave here today, you won't see us again until you call us because this office will close today. We haven't been here."

"Gentlemen, I'd like to thank you for the help you've given me and for this opportunity. I believe this job will take some time, but I can do what needs to be done. If there's nothing else to hold me here, I should be in New Jersey tonight so I'll say goodbye for now."

The last thing Jessie heard as he left was Gene saying, "Don't forget that phone number. It's your only friend and safe house if you call."

"I won't forget," Jessie said, "and thanks again."

Jessie had packed his car before leaving the motel so headed toward Richmond to catch Highway 95 to New Jersey. He decided to stop for the night in Wilmington and planned to drive through to Camden the next day. That night Jessie used his time to study the pictures and names associated with them. He memorized the phone number that was his only contact to the people he knew, and who were aware of his mission.

Chapter 6

When Jessie arrived in Camden the next day, he was surprised at how old many of the buildings and homes were. He planned to spend the day getting the lay of the land and rent a motel room until he could find an apartment. Once settled into his motel, he drove by a couple places and decided to grab a bite to eat at a restaurant called Sal's.

Once he sat down, he looked around and saw two of the men whose pictures he had studied. He was surprised at how fast that had happened. Once he had eaten, a waitress brought his check, but she was a different person than had originally brought him his food.

"Was your meal alright and would you care for some more coffee?" she asked.

Jessie was taken aback at how beautiful she was and uttered, while staring at her, that another coffee would be just fine. Her features indicated that she was probably Italian or very close. She had long, black hair that was probably shoulder length but was now worn in a ponytail. She was about 5'4" tall, and he guessed about 120 pounds of absolute beauty distributed in all the right places.

"The meal was delicious, and if you're just coming to work, I'll be back tomorrow at this same time," Jessie said.

She told him that the girl who had waited on him had to leave, and she was just filling in. "This is my dad's restaurant. Are you new in town?"

"Yes, I just got in last night. I'm Jessie Ruben. I just got out of the service so I thought I'd try this area for awhile."

"I hope you'll come back to see us when you get settled. My name's Francine, and my dad is Sal Uterio."

"If you're here, I will definitely be back."

As she walked away, Jessie couldn't help but look and admire what his mind and eyes told him was a great piece of work. He knew he'd like to get to know her better. He hadn't noticed a ring, but he couldn't believe that she could be unattached. Jessie vowed that he would find out more about this beauty in the very near future.

Chapter 7

It was still early so Jessie decided to drive to the other side of town and stopped at a place called Tony's Bar and Grill. Once inside, he had to allow time for his eyes to get accustomed to the darkness inside. He was surprised at how nice this little place was. It was like a small dinner club with a jukebox playing some quiet music. There was a place for a live band and a dance floor that some patrons were already using.

Jessie, now seated at one end of the long bar, could see a real big man sitting at the other end. He figured that the guy must be the bouncer, and not only that, but was a face among the pictures he had studied. As Jessie looked around, there weren't any other faces that he recognized so he drank the beer he had ordered and left to look over a couple other places.

He headed to Philly, PA and drove to the South side where there were two bars approximately four blocks apart.

At the first stop, a place called Jacko's Pool Hall, Jessie ordered a beer and took a look around. Several guys were playing pool and of the nine people in and around the area, a couple of them looked real familiar. Everyone appeared to be Mexican, Puerto Rican or black. This mix was usually fighting each other, but here, they seemed a peaceful group. Whoever got them together did quite a job 'cause with no fighting over territory, more money could be made by all. This could turn into one well-organized force as long as they could be kept as friends or partners.

With everything and everyone he had seen tonight, a plan was beginning to form in his mind. First, he had to know who was who, then draft a plan to get accepted by one of the bosses. Money was no problem so he could take his time.

* * * * *

With an idea for a plan in his mind, he allowed his thoughts to wander to Francine. He wondered if she was married or perhaps engaged. He truly wanted to know. No woman had ever made such an impression on him like meeting Francine and thoughts of her were constantly at the back of his brain. He had to know more. She had gotten under his skin in a matter of moments, but he came back to reality. He decided to cool it until he found out what her marital status was.

Before Jessie went back to his motel, he decided to pick up a newspaper so he could check listings for rental apartments. Once home, he poured over the classifieds and checked the listings that looked interesting. Tomorrow he would ask around and get input on the locations and the kind of areas they were in. He realized, as the evening went bon, that beer not only made you pee a lot, but also made it easy to go to sleep, which he did.

When Jessie awoke, after a great night's sleep, all he could think of was getting some breakfast. He remembered passing a place called *Mom and Pop Eatery* on the way to his motel from Sal's Bar. He picked up his newspaper and drove to the small but very clean looking eatery. When he went in, he was surprised that the place was packed with customers.

He was standing in the doorway when an older woman showed him to a table at the far end of the room. She asked him if he'd like some coffee, to which he nodded his reply. When she returned with his cup, she asked for his order and told him it wouldn't be long. While he waited, he looked around and thought, "Damn, this place is really packed like a truck stop. The food must be as good as the coffee." It took only a short while until he found out that the food was excellent, and his coffee cup never allowed to be empty. He was engrossed with his breakfast and didn't notice the attractive young woman approach his table.

"Well, I see you found the best food in town," a sweet voice said.

He looked up and there stood Francine from Sal's. He stood up and pulled out the chair on the other side of the table.

"Please sit down. I had no idea that you worked here too."

"No, I only come in to see my Aunt and Uncle about three times a week," she said. "They've been here for many years and have always done well because of the excellent food they serve."

"On that I have to agree," Jessie said. "Breakfast was top shelf so next I'll have to try their dinner."

"No, I'm afraid not, they only serve two meals a day and that's breakfast and lunch," Francine said.

"Well OK. I'll try that until I can find an apartment and do some of my own cooking. I'm glad you're here Francine because you know the different areas around here. I've checked off some apartments in the newspaper so maybe you could clue me in on the best locations."

She took the newspaper and looked at the places he had marked. "There are a couple here that might work for you. Both are on the East Side and that's the area we live in, and besides, it's one of the safest areas in town."

"Thank you Francine, I'll go look at those you've marked. Are you working today?"

"Yes, I go in around one o'clock to give my Dad a break."

"What does your husband do for a living?" Jessie asked her.

"Oh, I'm not married. My Dad says I'm too bossy and particular about who I date."

"I find nothing wrong with that. I know it's hard to meet someone special, but I've heard it said that you should just take your time and you will eventually meet the right one."

"When did you find your right one?" Francine asked.

"Haven't yet because, like you, I'm still single. I've been overseas and just got discharged so I haven't been looking yet."

"Mr. Ruben, may I ask you a personal question?" Francine asked.

"Ask away. I don't have anything to hide."

"Well, it's your name— Ruben. You don't look like most of the Rubens I've seen in the past. They were lighter skinned. You're more like me, with a darker complexion."

"Ruben is my adopted name. Both my adoptive parents have passed away. Since I've been a Ruben all my life, I saw no reason to change it."

"I hope no unpleasant memories have been brought up by my stupid question," Francine said.

"No, not at all. Although you're the first person I've told. I didn't know it myself until I read a letter left to me by my folks. I hope we can talk about this sometime in the future, but right now, I need to go look at these places so I can get out of the motel and get settled. I don't know what they'll look like, but you said they're in a good area. Thanks again for your help Francine. I might stop by the bar for dinner tonight so I'll let you know what I found. See you later."

Jessie left the restaurant and drove to a location on a tree-shaded street and parked in front of a well-kept duplex. His knock was answered by an older man who asked through the screen.

"What can I do for you young man?"

Jessie responded that he'd like to see the apartment that was advertised if still available. "Hold on a minute," the man said, "and I'll get the keys and show you the place." Together, they walked around to the other side and the old guy said, "Me and my wife live next door. We lead a pretty quiet life, and one of our rules is *no loud parties*. Are you married?"

By this time, they were inside the apartment, and Jessie replied as he looked around, "No, I'm single, just got out of the service and new in town. My name is Jessie Ruben, and like you and your wife, I also like a quiet place."

"Glad to meet you Jessie. My name is Lee and my wife's name is Pat. Lee and Pat Statler. We require at least a six-month lease. The man that was here before you was also single and lived here for almost three years until he got transferred to the West Coast."

"This place looks perfect for me," Jessie said. "It's got a lot of room and the furniture looks comfortable, so if you agree, I'll sign that six-month lease you require. When can I move in?"

"Jessie, once the lease is signed, you can call from my place to have the electricity turned on and move in anytime you want," Lee said.

With the paperwork done and a couple months rent paid, Jessie was surprised that the electricity would be turned on later in the afternoon.

"Thank you Mr. Statler. I'll move in this evening as all I have is one large suitcase back at the motel."

"Good, Jessie. Here are the keys, and you can park in the driveway on your side. Hope you'll enjoy your stay. Look forward to you being with us for some time."

Jessie drove back to the motel to retrieve his suitcase and checked out of the motel. There was plenty of time left in the day to check out some of the hangouts of the crew that he needed to get to know.

Chapter 8

Jessie decided that a good place to start would be the pool tables he saw yesterday in the bar. Later, with beer in hand, he sat down back where the tables were. The game on the first table was almost through. He asked if anyone had a winner for the next game.

Some guy answered, "No, looks like my pigeon has to leave so the next game is open."

"Then I'd like to try," Jessie said, "although you look like you know the game pretty good."

"Good, my ass, he's a hustlin' son of a bitch"!

"That's what I like is a good loser. See you tomorrow Joe."

While racking the balls, Jessie asked the guy what game he wanted.

"How about a game of straight pool to start with ten dollars on fifty balls?"

"Sounds good to me, and I'm Jessie".

"Glad to know you, I'm Kyle. Why don't you break so I can see how you play?"

Wanting to lose but not by too much, Jessie ran two racks before a missed cue shot that looked good. Kyle never knew it was on purpose. Before the game was through, Jessie had to miss a couple more shots.

While on their second set, the table beside them started getting loud. Looked like the losing guy was drinking too much and a few minute later when Kyle missed a shot, Jessie went around between the two tables to take his shot. Before he got set, the guy at the other table nearest Jessie said, "You cheating son of a bitch," and started moving toward the guy at the end of the table. The other guy didn't see the knife that was coming toward him. As he passed Jessie, his arm was grabbed; he was flipped backwards which made him drop the knife. His next mistake was swinging at Jessie who decked him with one smack. Suddenly the place went quiet as all eyes were on Jessie wondering what was next. Jessie picked up the knife and helped the guy to his feet.

"Sorry son, but you could have been in real trouble and this way, everybody goes home and no one goes to jail."

Jessie watched him stagger toward the door and resumed his pool shot. As he turned, the intended victim of the knifing was holding out his hand. "I know you're new here by what you just did, but that guy will remember you and try to get even. Do you have any friends around here?"

"No, I just moved here from Virginia and wasn't looking for any trouble."

"Well, you got some friends now," the man said. "I'm Jumbo and thanks to you, still here. You saved at least one life today and even if he didn't know it, his too. That's Harry over on the other end with Kyle. Both would have stopped him, but of course, too late for me. What are you doing in this part of the country?"

"Just looking for a place to settle. Met a guy overseas who said you could find a good paying job here if you knew how to keep your mouth shut, so here I am."

"Do you remember the guy's name? Maybe we knew him," Jumbo asked.

"Oh, he wasn't from here," Jessie said. "He said his grandfather talked about a family, Bulardi or something that sounded like that. He said it was a long time ago. Anyway, I got no one so I'll give it a shot and see what turns up."

"Who knows, maybe there's a job or two," Jumbo said. "I'll check around for you with a couple guys I know. How can I get in touch with you?"

"I'm getting a cell phone. Once I get the number, I'll drop back by here and leave the number with the bartender," Jessie said. "Do you guys come here often?"

"Yeah, this is like our second home, and we're here most nights," Jumbo said.

Jessie said, "Good, then I'll probably catch you here tomorrow after I get my phone, but now I've got to finish this game to I can get moved tonight." Jessie let Kyle win the last game and told them all he would see them tomorrow night.

* * * * *

What a stroke of luck he had just had. Jumbo was one of the men he had hoped to meet. This could be the way to get into the organization. Jessie looked at his watch and decided he'd head to his new apartment and clean up before going to eat at Sal's. He wanted to do a little inventory of what he'd need to settle in. He only had a towel and washcloth along with a few clothes and was delighted as he checked through the cupboards of his new place. In the hall closet he found towels, wash cloths, sheets and a blanket. The kitchen was stocked with pots, pans, and dishes. All he needed to purchase was the food to cook, and he'd be in business. He made his grocery list, took a shower, and headed out the door. He saw Lee and Pat working in the yard.

"Did you find everything OK, Jessie?" Lee asked.

"Sure did. It looks like all I need is some food; everything else is there. I sure thank you."

"Well, when we got married, both of us had furniture so we were able to furnish it with no trouble. If there's anything else you need, ask us before you buy something, 'cause we probably got one someplace."

"Thanks again, but from what I've seen, it has everything. Would you and Pat join me for dinner tonight?"

"No," Lee said. "We appreciate it but perhaps some other time, if you don't mind."

"OK, then one day next week," Jessie said. "I'd like to take you to a place I found last night called Sal's. The food was very good; in fact, that's where I'm headed now. See ya later."

Chapter 9

When Jessie got to Sal's, he didn't see Francine. Another waitress seated him near the back as he requested. He ordered a glass of wine before his meal. Looking at the menu, he didn't immediately notice that it was Francine who brought his wine.

"Hello," she said, "I saw you come in so thought I'd tell you about our specials today which I made as Pop went home to rest."

Jessie put down the menu and said, "Then by all means, that's what I'll have and find out if you cook as good as you look".

"Why thank you sir, I'll be out with your dinner shortly."

Jessie didn't have long to wait and had just finished his wine when Francine returned with a tray loaded down with food.

"I hope you like your meal," she said. "I've brought you two different dishes, both on the special but I wondered which one you'd like the best."

"If you'll sit down and have a drink with me, I can tell you in a very few minutes." Jessie took a bite of one and then the other. He told Francine it would take more time than he thought to decide which one he liked best because they were both delicious.

At the sound of a bell, Francine told him she had to get back to work.

"When you get a chance, come back and I'll give you an answer on which of the dishes was my favorite," Jessie said.

He totally enjoyed his meal and was just sitting back with an after-dinner coffee when Francine approached once again.

"Sorry I took so long but work comes first. Did the food meet with your approval?"

He looked at her, smiled and said, "Francine, that was the best food I've eaten in a very long time, except perhaps in Italy."

She was a little flustered because she knew she was a great cook and told him, "Ah yes, but I gave this my personal touch, so there!"

Jessie realizing he might have hurt her feelings said, "Don't you know you just took the words out of my big mouth? All joking aside, you can cook for me anytime Francine. In fact, do you remember those apartments that you marked? Well, I went to the one on Adam Street and rented a very nice place. I'm planning to bring my landlords here to eat one day next week. With food like you have prepared, it will be a big hit with them. I didn't mean to hurt your feelings, but perhaps I can make it up to you with dinner and a movie sometime if your parents don't mind."

"If we do go out, it's not up to anyone but me," Francine said, "although Dad would get a kick out of it if you were to ask him. Mom would have a million questions to ask you. Tell you what. You can ask my Dad. It would be fun to see his reaction because no one has ever asked his permission to date me that I know of."

"When you feel like you're ready to try dinner, dancing or a movie, let me know and I'll ask him," Jessie said.

"OK Jessie, thanks. Now tell me about the apartment you found."

"Well, it's a 2 bedroom, 1-½ baths, kitchen, living room and laundry room and is totally furnished right down to the kitchen utensils. It's a duplex and the owners are in the unit next door. The rent is far too inexpensive for what I have, but they wanted someone that would take care of it so they let me have it pretty cheap."

Francine told him she'd be very pleased to fix something special for them. With that, Jessie said his farewells, paid his bill, and left to buy the groceries to stock his new place.

Chapter 10

Jessie had put all his groceries away the night before, so had everything he needed to fix himself a nice breakfast. He was comfortable here. It felt good to have his own place instead of the displaced feeling a motel room can give you.

He decided to spend his day learning his way around the town and some of the territories which would certainly come in handy later on. He finished breakfast, cleaned up his cooking mess, and hit the road.

He stopped by one of the known hangouts and went in to look around. Here, as in the pool hall, he saw one group hanging together. They were talking low, and he couldn't hear anything. He had to pass their booth on the way to the bathroom so he decided to try that. All he heard was, "you know where to go so move out." Three of the guys left and three remained. Jessie went back to his table and within a few minutes, two of the three left and only the talker remained. When he too finally left, Jessie wasn't far behind. Trailing him proved easy as he drove a few miles, went into a business and then repeated the same procedure four times more in all areas of Philly. The last stop was a somewhat desolate area where the guy opened a gate, drove through, and then shut the gate behind him. Jessie couldn't follow in there so he drove back to Camden. He decided his next move would be to visit those places he had seen the man enter. Could be he was a bagman on a pick-up trip. By the way he had given the orders, Jessie was sure he wasn't one of the crew but some kind of boss. The information about all of the crews working together meant that this was a small part of a bigger gang. The question now was the gate he had gone through. It must have had a long driveway, as Jessie hadn't seen a house.

A phone call to his contact, Gene, would find out who lived there for future reference.

*   *   *   *   *

When Jessie arrived home he saw Lee working on his flower garden. "Hello Lee, looks like fun, need any help?"

"No, I'm just getting a few weeds out and them I'm through. How was your day?"

"Not too bad. I was doing a little sightseeing so I could learn my way around but I wanted to ask you what kind of food you and Pat like?"

"Well, you said Sal's Restaurant is Italian and anything Italian is good so I'd say anything they might serve is fine with us. Why?"

"The cook said if there was anything special you wanted, she'd be happy to fix it for you," Jessie said. "OK Lee, you guys decide when and we'll go. Right now I have to make some phone calls so I'll see you later."

Jessie wasn't sure that his cell phone had been turned on yet, but when he checked it out, sure enough, there was a dial tone. He dialed Gene's number, which was answered on the second ring. He told the voice on the other end what he wanted and was told to call back in one hour for the answer. Jessie hung up, fixed a sandwich, a cold drink and turned on the TV to kill some time.

When the hour had finally passed, he called his contact again and received his answer. The property belonged to Geno Industries, an amusement company which was owned by a corporation from Philadelphia.

"Do me another favor and send me a list of the stockholders or owners," Jessie said. He gave his address and hung up. Might as well go shoot some pool and see if Jumbo had done any good regarding a job.

He drove to Tony's Bar and Grill, walked in and saw that only two men were shooting pool near the back. One of the guys was Jumbo and the other the man that Jessie had stopped last night.

Seeing Jessie, Jumbo said, "Don't worry, Chico came to thank you for saving his life. One of his buddies finally got him sober and told him what happened so it's all good."

Chico came around the table with his hand outstretched to shake Jessie's.

"Believe me, when I came to my senses, I knew there would have been a lot of trouble without you so please, let me buy you a drink and thank you."

Jessie accepted the handshake.

"I'm glad we can be friends. It takes a big man to admit when he's wrong so I accept your thanks and a cold beer."

Jumbo put up the pool cues.

"Let's sit down at one of the back booths and talk a little."

The waitress brought them their drinks, and once she left, Jumbo said, "There may be a job for you if you don't mind starting at the bottom. My contacts like to know something about their guys before moving them up."

"Fair enough," Jessie said. "Ask anything and I'll try to answer. I'm not hard to check out as I've spent the last six years in the army and before that in school. All I need is a chance to prove myself."

"That's good Jessie," Jumbo said. "You know how to take orders so you got one leg up over others. Be here in the morning to pick up Chico for a drive to Atlantic City, then wait for him until he comes back. Here's your first paycheck."

Jumbo took an envelope out of his pocket and gave it to Jessie who put it in his back pocket without first looking at the contents.

They ordered another round and Jessie asked Chico "What time is good for you Chico and do you want me to drive? If so, I'll get gassed up."

"Yeah, you drive and around seven sounds good. One more thing I've got to know Jessie, where did you learn to fight like Jumbo said."

"Ranger training in the Airborne. They taught us a lot of things there."

"Someday maybe you could show me a little," Chico said, "so I could stop someone as easy as you stopped me. Jumbo's so big he just breaks their bones with his big hands."

"When you learn the art of self-defense, sometimes size works against you. About tomorrow, do I need to carry?"

"No, not this time unless you feel you need to," Jumbo said.

"OK, well if we're set, I'm going to go eat at Sal's," Jessie said. "Have you eaten there before?"

"Yes, a couple times," Jumbo said. "They have good food and the scenery is mighty good. I know you've seen Francine, and so far, no one has got to first base with her 'cause she's one tough broad."

"How about her dad?" Jessie asked. "He looks like he could be a bad ass."

"No, not Sal," Jumbo said. "But when it comes to the rest of his brothers, look out. Sal has always had a restaurant and in his family, Francine is the strong one."

"You're right," Jessie said, "But boy can she cook and besides, she's also the prettiest. I'll see you later, take care."

Jessie left Tony's place and drove to a service station to fill up for tomorrow's trip. He went on to Sal's where he could see Francine and have a good dinner. By this time of evening, the dinner crowd would be starting to leave so finding a seat wouldn't be too hard. Besides, he could sit at the bar until there was an opening which was the good thing about not being in a hurry. When Jessie walked in, he saw it was pretty crowded so he went to the bar and ordered a beer while he waited. As luck would have it, the bartender was Francine's dad. He brought the beer to Jessie and told him that because her aunt had gotten sick, she had to spend time with her but mentioned that Jessie might be in.

"I did want to talk to you sir," Jessie said. "When I know Francine a little better, I'd like your permission to ask her out for a movie and dinner."

"Francine marches to her own drummer and isn't bashful about telling someone to kiss off, Sal said. "As for me to say OK, you got it. Next, you have to get by her, and for that, I wish you luck!"

"Thank you sir, I really appreciate it. Now I think I see an open booth so I'll grab it and have dinner. Thanks again and goodnight."

Jessie placed his order for the special, and his thoughts turned to the job he had to do.

Chapter 11

Cut off the snake's head. Sometimes there was more than one person running an outfit this big. No problem, take them out one at a time. The small fry usually weren't smart enough to survive without a leader. That would finish his job but right now he had to play his cards close to the vest so he would be accepted and be allowed to move up. Sometime soon he would find out who owned Geno Industries and that would at least be a start.

Jessie didn't want to hang around without Francine there so he paid his check and drove home.

Little did Jessie know that the next day was a set-up to check him out. Chico left and came back with a large heavy suitcase.

"I got it," he said, "so let's get out of here."

He was surprised when Jessie asked, "Back the same way or change our route?"

"No, the same way; just keep your eyes open in case of trouble."

When they arrived back in Camden, Jessie asked, "Where do you want to go now?"

"Drop me off at that warehouse behind Tony's."

"You got it, what should I do?"

"Go someplace and come back to Tony's in a couple hours," Chico said.

When Jessie drove off, Chico walked back to Tony's but first, he emptied the bricks out of the suitcase.

Chico entered Tony's and met Jumbo there.

"Well, how'd he do?" asked Jumbo.

"Top notch," Chico replied. "Not one question about what I had and even asked about taking another way home. Let's make a real run and go from there."

"OK, I'll set it up for the real stuff in two days," Chico said. "When he comes back, I'm taking him to the Carry Inn Club. I want to see how good he really is."

"Ain't that the biker's hangout?"

"Yeah, they have more fights for fun than other people do for real. Some of those bastards can fight and while I'm there, I'll see Leo about his order so it looks like business."

Later when Jessie walked in, Chico told him they had to see a man about his order. It's a biker's bar called the Carry Inn, and it's one rough place. No one cares who you are so I may need some help."

"Sounds like it could be fun," Jessie said. "It's been awhile, so I'm ready when you are."

Chico said, "Let me finish my drink and we're on our way". Chico told Jumbo they would see him later and they drove to the outskirts of Camden to the Carry Inn.

When they parked in front of the building, there were quite a few motorcycles sitting around.

"I can see why this place is so far out in the boonies. Just listen to that noise!" Jessie said.

"Hell, they're just getting warmed up. The real noise is when they try to close, and all these bikes crank up. Be careful when we go in because someone may not like our looks. You can hit the bar while I go into Leo's office."

Getting to the bar was a job all by itself. Both walls had people standing, drinking and talking. The only clear path was between two pool tables. Chico passed with no trouble but as Jessie started around, a big man on his left drew back his pool cue to take a shot at a nine ball. When his cue came back, it hit Jessie in the side and caused the guy to miss. Needless to say, he wasn't at all happy.

"You no good son of a bitch," the man said. "You owe that guy fifty dollars that you just caused me to lose."

"Sorry about that," Jessie said. "Maybe you can beat him on the next game. This was the only way we could get to the bar with all those guys on the side."

"Never mind the bullshit. Give the guy the money or I'll stomp your ass!"

This was when the man as big as Jumbo made a bad mistake. He swung the cue he was holding at Jessie. The cue missed as Jessie ducked, and at the same time, Jessie's foot caught him square in the chin. Almost before it started, it was over with the big guy stretched out on the floor.

One of the other players said, "We got no irons in that fire, but Jacko will when he comes to."

"I hope not. All I wanted was a cold beer. I'd sure hate to hurt him any more." This said, Jessie walked to the bar and ordered a beer.

Meanwhile, Chico, who had seen the whole thing, went in to see Leo the owner.

"Is that guy with you?" Leo asked. "If not, I wonder if he'd want a job. That big son of a bitch he decked has been a real troublemaker, so tell your boy to watch out because he carries a knife and don't mind using it. That's why no one else got in."

While they were talking, the big guy got up and started toward Jessie. Watching him in the mirror, Jessie turned around and said, "Can I buy you a beer?"

"Yeah," the guy said. "As soon as I cut you up a little, you sneaky bastard, kicking me when I wasn't looking!"

"I hoped you'd have a beer and let it go," Jessie said. "Now you leave me no choice so turn your dog loose."

Once more Jacko made a pass at Jessie who sidestepped the knife, turned sideways, grabbed his arm and threw Jacko over his shoulder in what's called a double arm hand stand. Jacko laid on his back about nine feet away and before he could recoup, Jessie had the point of his knife on his throat and asked, "Do you want to play some more or should I end it here?" This was probably the only time you could have heard a pin drop because the place was so quiet.

"No, please, you win. I'd like to have that beer now if you still want to."

Jessie stepped back and helped Jacko up. He gave him back his knife and watched as he put it away. They went to the bar to have that drink. Then everybody was talking at once, and the noise returned.

Chico came out and told Jessie it was time to go so with a parting comment to Jacko of "take it easy" they left.

Once in the car, Chico had to say, "How in the hell did you do that? That bastard was Jumbo's size, and you cut him down without raising a sweat."

"Remember I said size can also work against you?" Jessie said. "Then too, a big man can be deadly if he uses his brain."

"You know today, you didn't ask what I picked up at our first stop. Weren't you curious?" Chico asked.

"None of my business. You'll tell me when I need to know."

"OK but how about where I went when I left you alone? Didn't you kind of worry?"

"Why should I worry?" Jessie said. "I hadn't done anything wrong, so what would I have to worry about?"

"Damn!" Chico said, "You are one cool mother and I like that. We're going to take another trip in two days so you have some fun until then. Now let's go back to Tony's."

Once there, Jessie told Chico he was going to Sal's to have some dinner and asked if he wanted to go with him.

"No," Chico said, "I've got to see Jumbo so you go. I'll call you if anything comes up before we take our next trip."

Chico got out of the car and went inside. He saw Jumbo and Joe playing pool at the back table.

"Well, I see you made it back in one piece, no trouble to speak of?"

"No, not really," Chico said. "Although Jessie had a little fun with a big S.O.B and never even worked up a sweat. That guy is a real bad ass, and he never gets shook up. I mean cool as a cucumber. This big guy, your size Jumbo, tried to hit him with a pool cue. No luck. Then he really screwed up and pulled a knife—and almost had to eat it. Then Jessie bought the bastard a beer! When I get in a fight, I'd like him on my side. About the job today. I asked him why he didn't say anything. 'Wasn't none of my business,' Jessie said, 'When it is, you'll tell me.' Don't that take the cake?"

"Sounds like he could be alright. We got Jacob Myers checking him out, you know the cop? So far he can't find anything and even some of his army records are sealed so he has a friend trying to get a look at them. Anyway, you're set up for tomorrow as we're running short of China White so it's back to the ship. This load goes to Gerry's in Philly. You know the house so go straight there 'cause the boss said all is well."

Chapter 12

Jessie headed to Sal's. When he got there, he went straight to the bar and saw Francine's dad working once again.

"Well, I see you came back, and she's here this time."

"I had hoped she was so I can tell her I asked your permission to take her out."

Jessie saw an open booth, walked over and sat down. Within a few minutes, she came out of the kitchen and saw him. She came over and asked him how he was.

"Francine, I'm more than fine because last night I asked your father, if after you know me better, could I ask you out. Guess what? He almost laughed before he said OK. Then he said it wasn't up to him as you made up your own mind."

"Yes, that's my Dad. Now one of my Uncles wouldn't feel that way. He'd say ask Dad first. Well, you did, now it's up to me."

"I didn't know you had an Uncle here."

"I don't, I have two. Both are in the wrong business and are not good people to know. By the way, what do you do for a living?"

"Well, in the army I did a lot of exterminating. Now I've done real well in the stock market so I hope to be a problem solver for a few months and then retire. What are your plans for the future?"

"I'd like to get Dad to sell out so him and Mom could retire and move away from here so I can start a business someplace else. This isn't a good place for someone with the name of Uterio to bring up a family"

"Ah yes, but you don't have any children yet."

"No, but I'll find someone who I want to be the father of my children, and if not, I'll be an old maid. Ha-ha."

"Then I can tell you that so far, you have tried the rest; now you can try the best. How does that sound?"

"Like someone is bragging or could be telling the truth; but there again, only time can tell. Now what would you like tonight for dinner?"

"Tonight, it's your choice, but tomorrow I hope to bring Pat and Lee in for you to meet. Then I'd like to go out with you, and please remember, your Dad said it was OK."

"Then I guess you win, but only the first round. Let me go get your dinner and something to drink."

When she returned, they talked while he ate.

"I'll be looking for all of you about six. Is that about right?"

"Yes, they're like me; don't want to eat too late. Once again the food is terrific so I'll see you tomorrow."

Jessie paid his bill and drove home planning to ask Pat if they were available for dinner tomorrow night. When Jessie reached home, he talked to Pat about the dinner plans. They agreed to leave at 5:30, and Pat added that a letter had arrived for him.

Once inside his apartment, he looked at the envelope with his address but no return address. He knew it was from his contact which read:

Chapter 13

The Uterio brothers, Salvador and Moriano, started Geno Industries. Now it is owned by stockholders. Also, here is a complete layout of the land and house. They also have a warehouse in Philly for their coin machine business which is legal but is also a front for their money-making operations.

There are three brothers; the other is also a Sal, Saloria. He is not in the business in any way we can find. Just watch your ass. Someone has been checking on you. There are some big people on the stockholder's list, and here are some of them.

After looking everything over again, Jessie destroyed all of the documents including the envelope they came in. The last to go was the layout of the house and land. He would now have to visit it but by the back way. Forming a plan he decided in the morning to take a ride by the warehouse to see what activity was going on. He would then take a drive and look over the land at the Geno Industries. His plans also included a night trip to see what was there. He wondered how close he could get to the house unobserved. Did anyone live there all the time? How often was it used and for what purpose? He remembered the layout of the house. There was a large basement under the three bedrooms and size-wise, only twenty four hundred square feet. Once he had carefully looked it over, a stakeout by him would be next.

Early the next day, he drove to the warehouse location and drove by slowly so he could see the warehouse and surrounding grounds. Near the warehouse were half a dozen blue panel vans with Geno lettering on the side. It looked like this was the legit part of the business. He didn't stop and drove past the gate he had followed the man to. He drove on down the road and saw a couple places he could hide the car off the road. Then out of sight at dark, he could check out the grounds. He wasn't able to see the house because of the trees and wondered about guard dogs which he'd find out the first night he had free and after the next run with Chico.

The road he was on continued way past the end of the boundary he was checking out. This was good also as after he passed the gate to turn in, he only passed what looked like a farmhouse set back off the road. Tonight after dinner with Pat and Lee, he would drop them off and see how it looked in the dark. With time to spare today, he would find a place to watch the gate.

Around four thirty, he called it a day as he had to get ready for dinner at Sal's. As he was driving home, his cell phone rang.

"Hello," he said, "Jes here."

"It's me, Jumbo. You have another job tomorrow. Pick up Chico like you did before. He knows where to go like last time so don't be late."

"No problem. Got a date tonight, but we'll be home early. Tell Chico I'll bring coffee."

"Good, I'll see you when you get back. We can talk about more work then, although it looks like you'll be a driver for a week or two."

"You're the boss so anything you need, I'm game. See you tomorrow."

Jessie arrived home, took a shower and dressed for the evening. With a little time left, he watched a little TV until it was time to leave. He locked his apartment at exactly five thirty, just as Pat and Lee came out of theirs. Jessie offered to drive and said, "I promise I'll get you home full and in one piece." They accepted and in fact were grateful, because they wouldn't have to take their car out of the garage.

When they arrived at Sal's, Francine was greeting another couple but spotted Jessie and his friends. As quickly as possible, she walked over to them.

"Francine, I'd like you to meet Pat and Lee Statler, the couple I told you about. This is Francine." They all greeted each other like old friends and then Francine led them to a booth and took their drink orders.

"Jessie told me that you like Italian food so I've prepared some special dishes for you that I'm sure you'll like," Francine said.

"I'm sure we will. Jessie has told us how good your cook is and how good looking."

"I'll have Ralph come out when he gets time. Ha-ha."

"Oh no," Jessie said, "I mean the one I asked to go to a movie, that's the one. Pat, this is the cook I was talking about. Her father is the owner of this restaurant."

Francine left to get their meals

"I see why you come here," Lee said as she left. "She is a knockout and if she can cook like you say, what a catch, and that's why I let Pat hook me!"

"You men are all alike," Pat chimed in.

Francine brought the food, and they totally enjoyed the variety—and ate until they were stuffed. When the word desert was mentioned, they all said it would have to be on another visit because they were all too full. With coffee all around, they talked a little while before they got ready to leave. Just before they left, Jessie said to Francine, "Please think about going out with me in the near future, like a couple days from now."

"When you find the movie we both will like, I'm ready. Mystery, love or adventure, I like them all."

"Then I'll see you soon with a couple choices from which you can choose. I hope to see you in a couple days as I'm taking a trip tomorrow but will be back the next day. Thank you for a wonderful meal. Pat and Lee will tell all their friends so you may get some more business. Until I see you again, take care of yourself."

Later, after dropping the Statlers off at their home, Jessie drove out to the house he was going to check out.

Chapter 14

As he drove past the farmhouse, Jessie noticed that it was dark like no one lived there. He passed what looked like a logging road which was quite grown over but he could still pull in and be out of sight from the road. He turned around and headed home. Soon he would explore that house; but for now, sleep was what he most wanted. Jessie set his alarm clock so he could get the coffee before he picked up Chico and then went to bed.

He actually awoke before the alarm rang. He got up, showered, and dressed with time to spare. He drank a quick cup of coffee and ordered two more to take with him. Chico was standing in front of Tony's bar waiting for him.

"Chico, I hope you haven't been waiting long," he said.

"No man, I just got here. I'm glad you got some coffee. I'm still asleep."

Once on the road he told Jessie to head for the same place as before. This time he passed where he had dropped Chico off the last time.

"Hang a right at the next light, and you'll see a restaurant between those big buildings. You can get a sandwich and beer while I'm gone."

When Jessie pulled up in front, Chico slid over to the driver's seat.

"Be back in about twenty minutes so take your time. I'll be close so don't worry about your car."

"No sweat. I've got good insurance and need a break from all that hard work. Want me to order a sandwich for you?"

"Yeah, in about ten minutes. Order me a turkey sub, then in five minutes a cold Bud. I should be back by then."

Jessie went by the warehouse, turned down the road beside it. Looking behind the restaurant and not too far away was the Atlantic Ocean. Unless the road made a hard right, it could run into the ocean. In one way, it didn't matter because the big men didn't handle the product; they only handled the money. He went into the restaurant and noticed there were only a few people there. He sat at one of the booths. When the waitress took his order, he also ordered for Chico and asked the waitress to bring his food when he came in. Jessie was on his second bottle of beer when Chico arrived. The waitress followed Jessie's instruction and immediately served him.

"That didn't take very long," Jessie said.

"No, they were prepared when I got there. Now we have to make a couple stops when we get home. Let me finish up here, and we're on our way." On the way out, Jessie paid the bill, and they started back toward Camden.

"Remember the club we went to? That's where we're headed first. This time I only make a drop and we take off, so you stay in the car."

"Tell Leo I'll come out and visit some night when I'm not busy," Jessie said.

Chico responded with "Be back in a flash" as he got out of the car.

What a crowd he had tonight. Must have been at least forty bikes and at least a dozen cars. Jessie thought, "I'll bet he makes a good buck on both the club and his other enterprise. In fact, the enterprise is the real money maker."

When his job here was over, a long list of places would be sent along with some names to the DEA, unsigned by him of course. I wonder how Francine would like living with Raymond Gulardi (his real name). He decided that once this job was done; there would be no more undercover work. Hell, we might get a bar and grill together. I could learn how to run the bar, and Francine could do the rest.

While his mind was busy thinking of her, the door opened, and Chico, carrying a small package, got in.

"Tell you what, let me drive as you've never been where we're going. There are a lot of turns so you can relax."

Considering the way he went, there were a lot of twists and turns, but in a short time, Jessie knew where he was. Right in front of them were the gates that led to the Geno house. Chico turned in and pulled up at a small house. This had to be where the other man came that he followed.

Beside the house was a small garage, and in front, there was a pond with a small boat tied at the shore. Once parked, Chico opened the trunk and removed a large suitcase. Then with the package he had gotten from Leo, he knocked on the front door and said, "I'll be right back." The front door opened, and a large man let Chico in.

Jessie started to walk a little bit and look around. Never going far, he walked down to the pond like he was interested in it. He didn't see or hear any dogs. He looked for cover to approach the house and determined it shouldn't be any trouble at all. Glancing back toward the garage, he noticed something sparkle as the front door opened, and Chico emerged. Jessie turned the car around and saw the camera mounted to cover all the front of the house. I'd bet money that they got it covered from all angles and probably some kind of alarm system as well.

"Where to next?" he asked Chico.

"Now to Tony's and a cold one."

"You know, that would be a fun place to live with that lake there. I bet that guy catches some great fish."

"Nah, no one lives there anymore. It's only a meeting place. Shooter won't be there too long. All he does is watch the place and have it ready when they all get together for one of their meetings."

"Sounds like a big crew."

"Only about five I think. Although we're never invited so I don't know how many or who they are. I just hear stories from Jumbo. A couple more runs and you will go by yourself. Next time I will take you in to meet people. Are you packing tonight?"

"Chico, I've always got something for back-up because you never know what some fool might do."

"What about using it? You any good?"

"Some day we'll go to the shooting range and see what you think. As far as using it, only when I have to, will I. Why?"

"We had a couple runners shot and their stuff stolen so thought you ought to know."

"Maybe that's why we make the big bucks. If it was so easy, he could hire some girls. Although I've known some who could probably do it and nobody who knew them would screw around. Any idea what Jumbo's got in mind?"

"He said we'd talk tonight so we'll find out soon as we've arrived," Chico said. "Park around in back as there's always more room back there."

Jessie did as he was instructed, and they were soon parked and going through the back door into Tony's. When they entered, they saw Jumbo sitting with some guy in the back booth. As they approached, the guy said goodbye to Jumbo and left as they walked up.

"Well, I see you both made it back. How was your trip?"

"Looks like our troubles might be over," Chico said. "This getting together with that other bunch seems to be paying off. No one else has been hit so it looks like the war is over for now. Never thought those bastards could ever get together. Now they have only one goon squad that handles all of our territory, and it takes only one visit from them and no more bullshit. They are some real bad asses."

"Did you guys notice that little guy who just left? That's the boss of those bad asses you talked about. One of his boys was there the other night when Jessie had that disagreement with the guy at Leo's. When he saw him with you, he wanted to find out who you were traveling with. He said he liked what he saw, but you didn't finish it—and gave him a chance to come back later. When his boys leave 'em, they can't walk for awhile. Also, he could use you if you want a change."

"Not now...I'm where I can learn from a guy that's been around and knows what might open up for me. Besides, I'd rather work with my brains than brawn."

"That's good thinking. Those assholes will always be used where they don't have to think. Now you and Chico will make some pickups so make sure you're packing some heat because a couple places you're headed are bad news. Some of those potheads think it's easy picking. Chico is known by these people so on the first two, you go in with him; the last two, you stay in the car. Next week we reverse the order so you'll be known. Day after tomorrow, you'll meet Chico here at 6 o'clock p.m. You both will be lookouts for a big meeting. Harry, Kyle and Joe will be on the outside; you two, the lake."

"Damn," said Chico, "What happened? They ain't had a meeting in two months since we all got together that night." " Who knows? When they say meeting, we jump. Remember Palo and Simms? They were too big to listen so they haven't been seen since that night. In fact, a couple more troublemakers must have taken a vacation because they're gone. Me, I'll keep my nose clean and play these games. After all, for the money we make, why make waves?"

"Jumbo, I have one question. Will you need me tomorrow night?

The reason I ask is that I have a date I'd like to keep."

"Oh-oh, and who is the lucky one?"

"I finally got Francine to go to a movie. I even asked her Dad."

"Damn, you are one lucky son of a bitch. Of all the guys who have tried, no one has got to first base. She doesn't take any crap from anyone. Nobody will screw with her because of her uncles so you watch your ass; they control a lot of people."

"They don't need to worry. I'll never hurt her in any way. There is just something about her I can't get out of my mind. How about one more drink before I hit the road?"

They signaled the waitress who brought them another round, which they quickly finished due to the lateness of the hour. As they parted for the night, Jessie told Chico to call him tomorrow when he was ready to go.

Chapter 15

Tonight he had a lot to think about. In order to capture the faces of those attending the meeting, he had to be at the lake with the infrared long-range camera, in a spot that couldn't be detected. He felt it was like history in the making. If nothing else, he could get the license plate numbers, and his contact could find the address for each car owner. Could this be a war council or just a way to plan what was to come? Somehow he needed to get a bug inside so he could eavesdrop on what was said and what plans were being made. So far, time had been good to him. Jumbo was trusting him more and more. From delivery boy to pickup man and now a soldier at a secret meeting. Who knew what he could find out within a month? Tomorrow he would call Francine to make sure she would be ready to go at 7 o'clock.

On the way home he stopped to buy a newspaper, mostly for the entertainment section. When he got home, he checked the moving listings. With so many choices he found one he thought they would both enjoy but would discuss it with her. Next, he pulled out his footlocker and checked some of the toys: everything needed to bug a house and take night pictures; two blocks of C4 with timer, caps and remote; one sniper rifle, two assault pistols with suppressors, one Mac 10, and a lot of ammo for all. "Don't think I forgot too much." he thought, but checked his belt holster Laser 38# and his snub-nosed 38 ankle holster. Now he was ready for a war of his own.

Little did Jessie know, but he was being discussed by Jumbo, a Cop on the force, and Leo who, as it turned out, was more than a bar owner. All of the men Jessie had met so far worked for him. Now he would be attending the meeting.

"What do you think?" Leo asked. "Can he be trusted? I've run him back to high school and so far, clean. The story from the Army is a bad ass but no stockade time. Some of his records are sealed for security reason, all overseas, and none in the states. Could be that's where he got his nickname. The only way they seal your record is for something bad or good they can't talk about. He said he came here 'cause some kid said his grandfather knew the Bulardis or something like that."

"Yeah, I heard that," Jumbo said. "The only one close to that was the Gulardis and that was a few years ago, all dead. That was when the brothers took over, and Jeno Industries was started. Back then they were two street punks. Look at them now, all respectable and in politics. They're the main reason no one screws with us."

"OK, he is your boy so keep an eye on him for awhile," Leo said. "So far he looks good, and he's sure not stupid. Chico said he looks right and never asks questions, so time will tell. Tomorrow he starts pickups; next week he'll go by himself, but never out of our sight."

Jessie realized that with his couple beers and the lateness of the hour, he was tired so he turned off the TV and went to bed. He got up around seven, showered, dressed and left to eat breakfast. There, helping the old folks, was Francine.

"Hello, looks like you've come to eat."

"Sure did! I was going to call you today but since you're here, why don't you pick one of these three movies. I'll be at your place at 7 o'clock unless you've changed your mind. You haven't, had you?"

"No way, since my dad said I could go. Here's my address and seven sounds good. Have a seat and breakfast will be right out. Oh by the way, do you want ham, eggs, sourdough and coffee?"

"You have read my mind, that's exactly what I wanted."

Before the food arrived, Chico called, and Jessie told him he had just ordered breakfast.

"That's OK; meet me in thirty minutes on the corner two blocks down the street from Tony's."

"I'll be there. Want me to bring you a coffee?"

"No, I can get one there."

After eating, Jessie told Francine he had an appointment but would be at her place by seven. He paid for his meal and left to pick up Chico.

He drove past Tony's per Chico's instruction and saw him

standing by the curb. Chico got in and said, "Hope that was a good breakfast."

"Sure was and I'd bet it was the best in Camden. Francine's Aunt and Uncle own the Mom and Pop Place, and she was there too."

"That takes the damn cake! You ain't been here any time, and I've been here twenty years, and I never knew that place was a restaurant. We'd drive by and thought it was a bar or something where old people hang out. Head for the East side and keep your eyes open. When you get to Main, turn right."

Jessie noticed they were entering a much seedier area and saw a group of young guys talking. "Stop in front of that place over there and don't worry about the crowd 'cause most of them work for us. Today you get to see one of our many businesses."

The building was similar to Tony's. They walked through to the back toward another door. Chico knocked, and the door was opened from the inside. Once in, Jessie realized they had just entered a very large bookie joint. Chico spoke to a few people as they continued through and finally entered a private office where two men sat at a table counting money. One of the guys said, "Got here a little early didn't you?"

"Yeah, got a new man so showing him around," Chico said. "Jessie, meet Clyde. He's the boss here so you'll be dealing with him." Clyde's hands were busy counting money so no handshake was offered. "We'll go have a beer until you get done."

"Good, I'll bring the bag out in a few minutes," Clyde said.

* * * * *

They went to the bar, ordered a couple beers and went back to one of the tables.

"We must have one smart boss to handle all these guys and run both businesses," Jessie said.

"Shit, you ain't seen nothing yet. We'll visit another joint like this and a couple trips today. We're the only two that handle four pickups. There are a couple more that hit other places. This is one big outfit. Tomorrow night, all the bosses meet for some reason; and since this is only their second meeting, we figure there must be something wrong."

"I've got a question," Jessie said, "How come you said bosses? Don't you mean top lieutenants?"

"No, all four of the families here in Camden and Philly found out that by working together, they split more money and have a lot less trouble which used to cost 'em. Before, we all stayed in our own territory. Now we go all over. Once they know you, you're as safe as a whore in church."

Just then Clyde came over to their table and handed Chico a paper bag that looked about half full.

"Who shall I look for next week?"

"Jessie here, but if something comes up, I'll be back. We might as well get on the road. Everybody should be up and moving by now."

Back in the car they drove only a couple miles to a little better part of town and parked at a large, two-story older home. A little old lady was sitting on the front porch. When Chico approached, she said, "Thought it was about time to see your smiling face."

"Hello Girt, want you to meet Jessie your new boy. He's going to take the run for awhile."

"Damn, I'd do him free anytime he wants. You're not from around here are you?"

"No ma'am, I came up from Virginia to see how life was in the big city."

"Hope you like it. Come back when you're not working and have a little fun."

"Thanks, I might take you up on that," Jessie said.

Girt handed Chico a small paper sack. They headed for another trip about four miles away and from there to a better-looking restaurant. Same as before. They went in the back where Jessie met a man named Troy. Jessie was watching the action and saw the money being passed around. After receiving a bag from Troy, he told Jessie he'd see him next week.

When they were on the road, Jessie asked about possible money shortages, the lack of count between locations, and the fact that there was never any verification whatsoever. Chico explained that each package is wrapped and put inside the bag in a certain way. They have other ways of packing, along with a signed amount of cash and number of bills.

"Believe me, it's not worth them or us helping ourselves. Now, head for the house by the lake so we can get rid of this."

When they parked beside the house, Chico took the four bags and with Jessie close behind, knocked on the door. It was Shooter who opened the door.

"Hello Shooter, this is a new guy and he'll make the next drops. Jessie, meet Shooter Walls, he looks after this place."

"Glad to know you Shooter. I like your job and with that lake full of fish, I'd be right at home."

"You like to fish? Maybe we could work out a trade? I need to leave a couple days next week so if you're off, you could watch the place for me. No one will be here so you can fish all you want."

"I could buy a rod and be ready in no time. What days are you thinking about?"

"I'll leave early Friday morning and be back Saturday night."

"OK, I'll ask Jumbo if he needs me. If not, I'll be here. We'll all be here tomorrow night anyway, so I'll let you know then."

"Good, that takes a load off me 'cause we like someone to be here so uninvited people are kept away."

"That's one job I can handle with no sweat."

"Are you done boy? I'm ready to take off," Chico said.

"So am I. I have to start getting ready for tonight. Got a date with an angel and sure don't want to be late."

"Now ain't that cute. I get you done in no time today just so you wouldn't be late and not even a thank you for all my hard work. Ha-ha."

Jessie couldn't resist the humor and said, "When we get to Tony's, I'll buy you a couple beers for your hard work." Later Jessie had the chance to talk with Jumbo and told him about taking Shooter's place at the lake for a couple days if he wasn't needed.

"What the hell do you want to stay out there for? Nothing to do but sit around and watch TV," Jumbo said,

"No, no," said Chico, "you are talking to a fisherman and that lake has fish in it."

"Jumbo, I've been overseas for the last four years," Jessie said. "I used to go fishing with my dad before I left. He died right before I came up here. This time would be for him as much as for me because he left before we could go."

"Next week is shot anyway with only a couple trips so you won't be missed," Jumbo replied.

"Thanks Jumbo, now I've got to leave and get ready for my date tonight. I'll see you tomorrow Chico so give me a call when you're ready to go." On the way out the door, he gave the bartender some money and told him to keep the drinks going for the guys.

The trip home didn't seem to take as long as usual because he had so much to think about. Being able to check out the house opened a lot of doors, like those cameras for example. Where were the receivers? Someone had to change the tapes once a day. With any luck, they were somewhere in the house. One thing was for sure. He would bring a few of his own toys and be ready for the next meeting. He already knew how to get them together for that. He would be ready to finish his job once it all came together.

Chapter 16

As he drove up his driveway, he saw Lee working in his flowerbed.

"Jessie, we want to thank you once more for a dinner to remember," Lee said. "That gal has everything a man could want, and on top of that, she's a hell of a cook."

"Some man will strike gold," Jessie agreed. "We're going to a show tonight, and if I play my cards right, maybe I'll get another date."

"From what I've seen of her, she has a strong will so you should let her in on what your plans are regarding her and your future plans."

"I do Lee. Otherwise she lets me know about it." Jessie laughed. "I really appreciate your advice because she's unlike any girl I've ever met. I would really like to get to know her better."

" Sounds like you plan to be here awhile. That's good, we like our renters to be happy."

* * * * *

When he got to his apartment, Jessie took a shower and dressed for his date. It was a little early so he turned on the news channel. There, as in other big cities, was what they thought was a drug-related killing of five people. They were found in a deserted farmhouse two miles out of Philadelphia. Looking at the picture of the dead men, there was one he knew from that first night when he saved Jumbo.

The man named Joe had been there. Now he was dead, but why? He wondered if Chico would know. At the end of the news report, he checked his watch and decided he would leave immediately which would put him only a little early at Francine's home. He was glad he had already driven by her house because he wouldn't have to guess about house numbers in the dark.

Chapter 17

He parked in front of the house and walked to the door and knocked. Francine opened the door and invited him in to meet her mother.

"Mom, this is Jessie Ruben, the man I told you about."

"How do you do, Mr. Ruben? I'm glad to see you're very punctual and polite enough to come to the door."

"Yes ma'am. I try to be and have always been somewhat old fashioned. I was taught that a lady should be treated with respect in all ways. In fact, if your daughter doesn't mind, you're welcome to join us this evening."

She thanked him but refused the invitation.

"Francine, I don't know where you found him, but I certainly do like this young man."

"Maybe he'll come back sometime mom," Francine said, "but right now we have to leave to make that first movie."

"Please come back again Mr. Ruben when we can talk for awhile."

"Thank you ma'am, but please call me Jessie."

As they left, Jessie said to Francine, "Did you pick us a good one?"

"You gave me a couple choices so I picked a comedy. It seems that there's not enough laughter in life anymore."

" You made a good decision because that's the one I most wanted to see too." Jessie wasn't very familiar with the theatres so he asked her which one they were going to.

"It's at the Bijou on Main Street," Francine replied. When they purchased the tickets, Jessie suggested they get some popcorn and drinks and requested extra butter on the popcorn. As they headed for the balcony, he asked her if she would mind sitting upstairs. She shook her head "no" meaning that she didn't mind at all. They easily found good seats, as there was little crowding because most people went to a later showing.

Once they were seated and enjoying the popcorn and sodas, Francine realized that she was very attracted to this handsome man sitting beside her. She wondered why he didn't make a move on her, not even putting his arm around her shoulder. She wondered what was wrong with her. Other guys she had dated always tried from the beginning to get to first base with her. She decided that she would have to make the first move. When he put his hand on the armrest, she did too. As they touched, she gave his hand a light squeeze, and he returned her touch with his own. When she didn't pull away, they continued to hold hands. However, as the movie continued, he didn't try to pull her close or try to kiss her. She was confused, despite the fact that she always hated those guys putting the moves on her before. This was different; she really liked Jessie. He was just sitting there which made her wonder if there was something wrong with her as no one had ever acted this way before.

When they walked to her door, he told her he had a wonderful time and would like to take her to dinner and dancing.

"I'd like to hold you but don't want to upset you by moving too fast. It takes time for people to get to know each other." She responded with "then I believe you should kiss me goodnight and ask me once you decide when and where."

Opening his arms, she came willingly into them. As their lips met, he could feel her breasts against his chest. The kiss was long and deep with an intensity that touched them both. He had to restrain himself from picking her up and carrying her to the softness of the summer grass. Keeping his passion in check, they parted and said goodnight. Francine stepped inside the house and closed the door. Jessie let out a breath of hot air. Once she was safely inside, he realized he would have to go home and take a cold shower.

Francine closed the door and stood with her back against it. There had never been a person or a kiss that affected her the way. Jessie and his kiss made her Italian blood run hot. It was hard to imagine dancing a slow dance with him and wondered how she could restrain herself once in his arms again. She wondered if he felt the same way.

* * * * *

Meanwhile, Jessie got home, and all he could think of was Francine. He was concerned that perhaps he came on too strong with that kiss but knew she had returned it. He decided that no time should be wasted in finding a nice dinner club so he could ask her out again. The trouble was that now all he could think of was her and their kiss. She was different. He was attracted to her in a way he had never felt before. It wasn't just about the passion but about the beautiful and kind woman that she was. He wondered if it could be love. All this thinking was getting him back in trouble; he decided to take that cold shower. In the shower, his thoughts finally changed to another matter. It was about Joe so he'd have to ask Chico why Joe had been there.

Jessie finally went to bed but rose early and headed for the Mom and Pop restaurant for breakfast. Francine came in as he was eating and sat down at his table.

"Just wanted you to know mom and I would like you to come to dinner tomorrow night around six thirty…if that would work for you."

"Tell your Mom I gladly accept. That must be where you learned to cook."

"Not really, she's good, but Dad is the chef in the family. I believe he has forgotten more than I know. By the way, have you found any work yet?"

"No, still looking. I'm in no hurry. There's a couple I may look into but don't think I'd like selling on the road. A consultation job on wilderness training might come open and that's something I would really like."

"I'll tell mom you'll be there for dinner. Right now I've got to relieve Pop so he can go to the doctor. See you at six, if not before."

Chapter 18

Jessie left shortly after Francine and decided to drive to Tony's bar. There, playing pool by himself, was Jumbo. "Looks like you beat all the competition and have no one to play with."

"Grab a cue and let's play a game of straight pool. First one to fifty wins. What're you doing here early? Did Chico call?"

"No, I didn't have anything to do so I hoped someone was here to play with. Besides, I need to get a lot better so I can win once in awhile." Jessie racked the balls.

"Some kid's grandfather told you about a family here called Bulardi," Jumbo said. "Never heard of them, but there was a family called Gulardi. They were pretty big in these parts at one time. I don't know what happened, but they were all killed and not long after that, the Uterio brothers started taking over."

"You mean Francine's dad, Sal?"

"No, Sal has never had anything but the restaurant. His two brothers are the ones who run Jeno Industries, among other things."

"How big was that family that got killed?" Jessie asked.

"I don't know how many. The old man's name was Raymond, and I think he had three sons, one daughter and two or three grandchildren. They were all murdered except one son and his wife. They got away but only for a little while. The story is they had a baby that was never found. You know how these stories keep the mystery alive. Well, the kid's granddad was right; at least they were here. Let's see the big break on a good tight rack."

Breaking the balls stopped the talk of the Gulardi family. Maybe he should ask Shooter if he heard the story. Some of the old crowd might know a little more about what happened. Jumbo won the first game; Jessie the second. They were about to start a third when Chico walked in and sat at the booth beside the pool table.

"Saved me a phone call," said Chico. "Who's winning?"

"Jumbo is. He's only playing to practice; but hell, I'm trying to win but no use."

"You know," Jumbo said, "I don't think I'd play him for real money. Some of the shots he made says he can play pool."

Jessie said, "I've played a lot and with practice, could play better. I never play for money, only beer or drinks. Money makes too many enemies of friends. When do you want to cut out tonight?"

"We should be there before dark to make sure everything is set up, probably in about an hour from now. Why?"

"Thought we could grab a sandwich to take with us 'cause I haven't eaten since breakfast."

"OK, we'll hit Subway when we leave here. Looks like the big man got you. All he needs is three balls."

"I hope so," Jessie said. "I'm getting tired after almost five hours. You can have him next."

"No, I'm with you, that's a lot of pool at one time. Let's sit down and have a cold one."

With a drink in front of each one, Jumbo said, "There was some trouble yesterday so you got a guy from Flo's to take Joe's place. Somehow he got dead yesterday. I don't know any of the details so can't give you any more info than that. You boys watch your ass until I find out what went down."

"Sounds like trouble in paradise," Chico said. "Maybe that's what the meeting is about. Somebody set it up, but why Joe was there is beyond me."

Jessie was trying to act uninterested so he sipped his beer and never got into the conversation. Chico reached into his pocket and pulled out his car keys.

"Here Jessie, take my car keys and put that bundle into the trunk while I go pee; then we should take off. I'll meet you outside at the car."

This gave Jessie an opportunity to hook up the camera he was already wearing. It was very small and took pictures that, from a distance, would have to be blown up to enlarge the image on it. Still, whatever came up, he should get some good shots. He loaded the bundle from Chico into the trunk and noticed the assault pistols and shotguns, two of each. So he was furnished the weapons to guard the bosses.

"If you're ready, let's hit that Subway," Chico said. "You've got me hungry for one too." They each ordered a footling and a couple drinks to take with them. "Hell, we'll get there in plenty time to eat. They won't come until it gets darker in case someone is following them. If that happens, our boys will stop them at the gate; and any that get through, belong to us. Pull over beside the pond but leave enough room for them to park. You take this side, and I'll be over by the side of the barn. After we eat, it will still be light so we can walk the area to check it out. I'll tell Shooter we're here so he can turn off the alarm."

"What alarm?" Jessie asked. "All I see are cameras."

"They have some kind of system that when you cross a certain area, the man in the house hears it."

"Now that's pretty damn smart. Somebody around here actually had a brain."

Once Chico told Shooter they were there, he turned off the alarms and came out to see Jessie.

"I'll see you Thursday night or Friday morning. Your call Shooter," Jessie said.

"Early Friday morning would fit the bill. That gives me plenty of time."

"OK, see you around six am, if that's not too early?"

"No, that's perfect and I'll have the coffee on."

"Good, see you then, but for now I'd better get to work."

Chapter 19

Jessie decided he'd better have a look around and get the lay of the land. When he got back, he told Chico that everything was clean and green. He didn't even see an animal.

"Try to find a comfortable place to wait until you see them come in; then just stay out of sight," Chico said.

"Don't worry. I've got a tree already picked out, and they won't see me unless you call."

How sweet it is, thought Jessie. From the fork in the tree, he had a straight shot at the front door and could get some great pictures of them coming out if he missed them when they went in.

When it was just starting to get dark, the first car arrived. As Jessie watched, he saw a man he had seen before, Leo. "Well I'll be damn, this is a surprise." It wasn't long before two more cars pulled in. As they got out and went to the door, Jessie got the pictures he had hoped for. So far, only Leo had driven himself. The rest had a driver. When the last car pulled up, two men got out of the back, and Jessie figured these must be the brothers. When the door closed behind them, all he could do was wait and think.

Someone had said there were four bosses. The brothers must be counted as one because if not, there were five. He decided that tomorrow, he would FedEx the film, along with the license numbers to his contact. In turn, his contact would send them back and he could see them Saturday. Friday would have been better but he wouldn't be available for the FedEx delivery.

Just as his mind started wandering toward thoughts of Francine, the bosses came out and got into their cars and left. Each had what looked like the same briefcases they had carried in. The thought occurred to Jessie that there had to be another drop-off point considering the extent of the territory. There had to be a bagman who picked up monies left here and delivered to the bosses. Was this the only meeting place for the bosses? Maybe Shooter would know, and if he asked in the right way, perhaps he could find out.

When the last car left, Chico got in the car.

"Well, how hard was that?"

Jessie responded with, "Wish I had brought my rod and reel, and I could have wet a line."

"I'll be glad when Friday comes so you can catch us enough fish for a fry," Chico said. "What say we go back to Tony's, and I'll buy you a cold one. By the way, did Jumbo tell you we've got a run tomorrow? It'll take about five hours 'cause we're going to Wilmington, Delaware, to pick up some stuff."

"No problem. If we leave early, I can still make my dinner date with time to spare." Jessie dropped Chico off after telling him he had an errand to run so he would be ready for his date. Jessie went back to his place, got the film ready to send and checked his toys. He made sure to include the remote with his C4 package and along with his listening bug, put them in a small carrying case and headed for the shower. Once out of the shower, he felt relaxed and decided to watch a little news before turning in.

Chapter 20

When dawn broke, Jessie was already on his way to meet Chico. His cell phone rang ten minutes before six and it was Chico. "Where you at, I'm waiting!"

"Where you at?"

"I'm here but you're not, why?"

"Damn, I'll be there in five minutes."

"You are right good for a Gringo, always on time, no questions and a little tough too."

"So that makes a good Gringo? I thought only a dead Gringo was a good Gringo."

"Si, but sometimes, it depends on how tough he is."

"How about some coffee while I get gas, then we're on our way."

Once on the road, they hit the Jersey turnpike and were there in no time at all. They crossed the Delaware Bridge, turned left on Highway 49 and drove through the town of Salem to the docks where Chico told him to stop. Tied close was a small schooner, and Chico went on board. He disappeared below deck and soon appeared carrying a large suitcase and a fully packed duffel bag. Behind him, another man carried the same type bags. They came directly toward the car so Jessie got out and opened the trunk. Once the bags were loaded, the other guy went back on board the schooner and started to weigh anchor. Jessie and Chico pulled away from the dock and headed back towards the Delaware Bridge. Once they got outside Camden, Jessie asked Chico where they were going now.

"To Jeno Industries, around and behind the small building on the left. Pull up to that door and give me the trunk key." Jessie waited in the car while Chico carried the bags into the side door.

As he climbed back into the car he said, "Day's work is done, let's go see Jumbo."

"I see you still have those guns wrapped up in back, do you want to leave them there until the next meeting."

"Why not, they 'ain't going nowhere."

"Chico, I've got a question for you. Does Jumbo live at Tony's? He's always there."

"Jumbo goes with the barmaid, and they aren't married so he hangs around there when she's working. Besides that, Tony's place is his office. All pick-ups go through him. We're only two of his men. There are three more teams so he has a big responsibility to the bosses.

When they got there, Jumbo was sitting in back talking to the barmaid. She went behind the bar to get the drinks.

"Looks like you made good time. Any trouble?" Jumbo said.

"No, not a hitch and we didn't see one cop."

"Was all the stuff there?"

"Yes, two suitcases and two duffel bags. Once we left, they left."

"After today's work, you boys take a few days off and have some fun. See me again next Tuesday." He handed them each an envelope and said, "Here, you guys earned this." With that, more drinks were ordered.

Once Jessie had downed his second beer, he said, "This has to be my last one. I have to go eat with the Uterio family tonight." Jessie didn't miss Jumbo's startled look so he said, "I'm having dinner with Francine and her family. I don't even know what the uncles look like. From what I'm told by her, I don't want to know. She doesn't think much of them but that's up to her. They're relations."

"Just remember," Jumbo said, "they rose awfully fast so don't screw up and get them after you. This place ain't big enough for you to hide. With their money and connections, they would hunt you down. That's why Sal's restaurant and the other Mom and Pop's haven't had any trouble. People know what would happen."

"I sure don't plan to make anybody mad. As far as Francine goes, I'll never hurt her in any way. When or if she ever tells me goodbye, I'm gone. Right now, I'm on my way to get ready. You boys be good and Chico, call me."

When Jessie was in his car headed home, he called his contact and got the address where he could send the film. He told him to trace the license plate pictures for addresses as well. He informed him he'd be gone Friday but would be home Saturday night. The Statlers will sign for it so I'll get it that night."

Jessie got home and decided to take a quick shower and shave. He had a little time to spare so sat back to relax and reflect over the day. Sweet thoughts of Francine began to enter his mind.

Chapter 21

Prompt being his nature, Jessie arrived at Francine's at six thirty sharp. She was sitting on the porch swing, and he noticed looking quite beautiful. She stopped the swing and motioned for him to sit down.

"Dinner isn't quite ready so I thought that perhaps we could talk for a few minutes," she said. "How is your job hunting coming along?"

"Like I told you before, I'm thinking about going into business somewhere. Maybe a Bar and Grill down in the Virgin Islands, but I can't run a restaurant. I'd need help with the bar so I have to find a beautiful Italian girl to help me. What do you think of a plan like that? Remember that money is no problem. That's why I'm in no hurry to take a job until I'm sure that girl would like that kind of life or isn't available."

"I guess I asked for that. It's really none of my business to be prying into yours."

"Francine, you asked and I told you. Maybe a different location or a different business, but I was serious about the girl. In a month, when you get to know me better, perhaps you could give me an answer on how you feel I've been doing. You think that's a possibility?"

She tried not to let him know that she understood whom he was talking about. She said, "Sometimes it doesn't take that long. With my luck and me so far, it took a lot longer. I think dinner is about ready so let's go in. If you don't mind, talk with my dad while I help mom.

Jessie followed her into the house and saw her dad watching TV.

"Dad, can you keep Jessie company while I help mom?"

"Sure can. Jessie, how about a glass of wine before dinner?" Without waiting for a reply, he asked Francine to bring them a glass of wine.

While they waited, her father said, "Jessie, I don't know what you've done to her, but I like it. She seems more relaxed, more cheerful, and less solemn than I've seen her in such a long time. Even her mother has noticed the positive changes so whatever you're doing, keep doing it."

"Why thank you sir. I really haven't done anything in particular. My intentions are honorable both toward her and her family."

"Then we are in you debt, for your inteentions, as you say."

Francine came back into the room carrying a tray with three glasses of wine, having caught just the tail end of their conversation. As Jessie rose to accept the glass from her, she smiled and said, "I hope you two weren't talking about anything important."

"No, nothing important," her dad said. "Just the weather and how Jessie likes it here."

"And did he tell you what he's looking for?"

"We hadn't gotten that far and besides, I hear mom, so let's go eat. By the way Jessie, how do you like that wine?"

"It has a nice flavor but different from any I've ever had before."

"That's because it's a wine and beer mixture. It's been around for a long time here in Camden, but most people don't know it."

Just then, Francine's mom called everyone to dinner. Jessie looked at the table and said, "There must be a lot more people coming to dinner with all the food that you've prepared."

She laughed and said, "Francine told us you're a good eater. Papa is not timid when it comes to eating, so please, sit down and enjoy."

After Papa said the blessing, what seemed like an endless amount of food was passed around for them to feast upon. Jessie didn't realize how much he was eating until he saw the beaming, smiling face of Francine's mom. She had noticed how he seemed to appreciate her cooking and she said, "Are you sure you're not just a little bit Italian?"

"Yes ma'am, I think I am but don't tell Francine." He couldn't help but laugh and said, "Someday I'll surprise her."

Francine chimed in and said, "Oh no you won't 'cause I asked you and you said No."

"Well, I don't know for sure because I was adopted as a baby.

Maybe someday I'll find out who my real parents were. When I settle down, I'll start my search. Maybe in a couple months when I decide where and with whom I want to begin my new life. Now, I'd like to apologize for being such a pig, but in all fairness, it was your fault for making it so good that I couldn't stop eating."

Mama's smile grew as her husband said, "Look at the good job I have done, showing her all my secrets. Now she is as good as me so I'll put her to work so I can quit and play golf."

"Yes dad, I want you to stop working so you and mom can enjoy your lives. Money is no problem, and you could sell out and move where it's warm all year 'round, perhaps Florida or out West. Mom's family is talking about doing the same thing. Then I too, could leave this place, and all the bad memories of our name being dragged through the mud. I'm sorry dad, I shouldn't have said that. They are your brothers, but not my uncles and not mom's brothers-in-law. They are related in name only."

Mama, sensing the tension said, "Francine, why don't you and Jessie take your coffee out to the porch swing while dad helps me clean up the dishes. Dad doesn't mind, and you have a guest, so go on now."

"OK mom. Come on Jessie, I'll carry the coffee out." Jessie opened the screen door for them, and once they were seated on the porch swing, Francine apologized for her outburst. "I'm so sorry, but I just hate my uncles' lifestyle and how they earn their money. I know they're guilty of many bad things, and I was just a baby when they first started work at their machine business. Mom said they really changed when that family was all killed."

"Did they ever find out who killed them?"

"I don't think so. Although mom said that Jeno Industries got really big, almost overnight. Some said they took over what the other family had. People believe they either had them killed or did it themselves, but no one dares to say it out loud."

"Tell me Francine, if your family doesn't sell out, will you ever leave here?"

"Yes, I think so. If I were someplace else, they would come for a visit, and I could show them what they're missing."

"If that's the case, I can only pray that we'll both find what we want. Speaking of that, have you given any more thought about going out for dinner and dancing in the near future?"

"Yes, I have given it some thought, and I would love to go. I can't even remember the last time I went dancing. It would be fun."

"Good. If Saturday would be OK, I'll pick you up around seven, and with a laugh added, should I ask your dad again?"

"Very funny! After what he said when you first got here, you know what he'd say."

"Well, if your mom and dad like me, maybe some of it will rub off on you. I don't have anything else working for me so I need all the help I can get."

"Did it ever occur to you that maybe you don't need any help? Have you thought about that?"

"Francine, I have thought about that, but I've never dated a girl that I wanted to get to know better until I met you. When I was in the Army, I was always on the move so there were never thoughts of one special person. Now that I've met you, I know you're the one girl I've always hoped I'd meet someday."

Jessie stood up and said, "Well, tomorrow is another work day for you. Please tell your folks how much I enjoyed the dinner and fine company." They moved toward the steps, but when he stopped to turn around, she stumbled forward and was caught in his arms. She didn't try to move away but was caught up in the kiss they shared. For Jessie, it was a kiss he would long remember as he held her soft, yet firm body in his arms. Like him, she felt a rapid surge of passion that almost made her head spin. Gently he moved back knowing if he didn't, he would never want to let go. A small gasp escaped her lips along with a nervous giggle, and all she could say was "whew."

Jessie backed down the steps and said, "Francine, thanks again for inviting me over tonight. I'll see you Saturday night at seven. Good night."

Francine was overwhelmed from the kiss and the all-encompassing feelings that came with it. She didn't move from that spot until Jessie's car lights were gone from her view. When she finally came to her senses, she picked up the coffee cups and walked back into the house to the kitchen. Her mom took the cups and said, "Now that you're back, dad can go back and watch some TV."

"Thanks daughter," he said, "has my little girl finally found a keeper?"

"Now dad, we don't know how he feels yet." Mama piped in and said, "Watching you two making calf eyes at each other, does make one think it could be getting serious."

With that, they all laughed together, hugged each other, and knew how wonderful it was to be a loving family.

Chapter 22

Jessie was trying to keep his mind off Francine, which was difficult for him to do. He knew tomorrow was a very important day. Was he forgetting anything? He could see where they had their meeting by the way the furniture was set up. That's where his "bug" would go. As far as the other "toys" were concerned, he would decide on the best location for them when he got there. Again and again he went through his plan and liked it. Of course, it all depended on getting them all together which he didn't think would be a problem. He was finally satisfied that nothing else needed to be done so once again, he let himself think of Francine.

There was no doubt in his mind; he was falling in love. Judging by the way that his kiss was returned, she had some feelings for him. He figured that Saturday night would be the right time to determine if she really cared as much for him as he did for her. With good thoughts of her in his mind and knowing he had to get up early, he went to bed and was soon asleep.

* * * * *

He woke early and after a shower and quick shave, drove to a fast food place to grab a breakfast sandwich and coffee, which he devoured while driving to the house. Jessie noticed that the gate was closed but not locked; so once he parked, he closed the gate. Shooter was already there and had a pot of coffee going. Just as Jessie entered the kitchen, Shooter was pouring them both a cup.

"Thought we could go over the only job I need you to do. Bring your cup and let's go downstairs."

As they descended the stairs, Jessie's eyes didn't miss a thing. Once at the bottom he saw a large table surrounded by chairs in the middle of the room. On the far end wall were the monitors.

"I changed the tapes this morning so you can do it tomorrow and leave them where the blank ones are."

"Tell me Shooter, do you ever see anyone on those tapes?"

"No, not since we put up those alarms. Pretty soon we're going to shitcan these. When I leave, I'll lock the gate so you won't have to. I'll be back around four Saturday."

"Shooter, can I ask you about the Gulardi family? Jumbo told me they were here a few years ago."

"Yeah, I knew them real good. I worked for them until they got shot. In fact, this place was theirs until Hal and Mel Uterio took over their business. Old man Raymond, the head of the family, was good to his people. Someone wanted to get ahead fast so the family was taken out. I'm just a soldier, but not stupid so I went along with staying here and being a guard. I'm not sure who pulled the triggers, but I have a good idea. Now, if you're as smart as I think you are, I'd forget this and any other talks. Just the mention of that name puts some on edge."

"I saw five bosses come in the other night. Hope you all had a good meeting."

"They may have, I don't know. See that back door? When they come in, I go out until they call and tell me it's over. I don't know nothing, don't hear nothing, and don't ask. Someday, it will all come home to roost. Who knows? The story is that one got away, girl or boy. They may come back to avenge their family. Oh, one more thing, the alarm system. Come in here to the front room. If you hear a beeping sound, look at the screen, and it will show you where the beam has been broken. Hit that switch on the right to turn it off. Then to re-set it, hit the switch again, and the beeping will stop. That's the whole job. No one should be here until I get back. When you fish, don't go too far so you can hear the alarm if it goes off. Well, I'm gone. Have fun and I'll see you Saturday."

"You take care, Shooter. I'll save you some fish if I catch any."

Chapter 23

Jessie gave Shooter plenty of time to leave the property and then went down and took the tape out of the camera on the front. Then he ran to the car and got his bag of toys. Once back in, he inserted the tape back in. This way, no one could see what he brought in. He looked around the basement and found a good place for his two remote bombs. On the far side was a furnace that hadn't been used for a good while. The other end had an air vent that would hide the second one. He noticed a large antique lamp hanging over the table and decided that it would perfectly conceal his "bug" with no problem at all. Then he went back to his car to get his fishing gear, which would be seen on camera.

Now to see about some fish. For the next two hours, he tried casting out with a jitterbug artificial bait, but all he caught were four small mouth bass. Looks like the big fish were farther out so he decided to try again in the morning or later tonight when it cooled down.

He had forgotten to ask Shooter about food so decided to check the kitchen. He saw a small freezer beside the refrigerator and looked in and was surprised to find that there was plenty of meat of all kinds. Then he checked the fridge and the whole bottom shelf was nothing but beer; the rest of the shelves were stuffed with all kinds of goodies. At least he had plenty to eat and drink. He fixed himself a sandwich and grabbed a couple beers and went into the front room to eat and watch TV.

He couldn't help but wish that Francine were here with him. He wondered if she had ever been fishing? Did she like the water and what about sports? There was so much he wanted to know about her. Tomorrow night they could talk about all those things. He wondered what she would think if she knew what his job really was. After all, two of those on his hit list were her uncles. There was only one way to be sure she would be alright with them being gone; he would never tell her he had anything to do with it. Still, what would she do when he told her his real name was Raymond Gulardi? When they left here and if they did get married, he was planning to use his real name, then settle far away but her people would know. That might put her in danger. The question now was to tell or not to tell. How much did a name mean compared to having her?

He had been Jessie Ruben as long as he could remember. If he didn't tell them any different, he still would be. Raymond Gulardi would stay dead as long as he had a chance with Francine.

His attention came back to the television and the news report of a couple killings that were said to be gang related. Tony's bar had been robbed, and a couple customers killed. No names were given pending notification of next of kin but who could it have been? They did say a man and a woman and the bartender were in critical condition at the hospital.

Whoever pulled this job had to be from someplace else. No one messed with a club where people like Jumbo hung out. That's like robbing a bookie joint that's protected by the people who run it.

He decided he'd go by there when he left. Wait a minute, he could call Chico on his cell. When Chico answered, Jessie asked, "What happened at Tony's?"

"Jumbo and his girl were sitting at their booth when a guy came out of the head and shot them both. His partner shot the new bartender, grabbed a few bucks and left. No witnesses. Sure looks like a setup. But who was mad at Jumbo?"

"Maybe two hopheads needed some money and didn't want to be recognized."

"I hope that's what it was. How's the fishing?"

"Well, I tried a littler earlier but only got a few small ones. When it cools down, I'll try again. Looks like I could use some live bait or need to go out into deeper water. When Shooter comes back, I may try then or some other time when he's here."

"OK, when you go home, hang loose until I find out what's going to happen next."

"I'll be home Sunday morning. I've got another date Saturday night."

"With the same broad, or another one?"

"No, the same one and I kinda like her. Not only is she good looking but a dynamite cook as well. She's the type of girl you would like to take home to meet the family. Seriously though, please call me if you find out what happened at Tony's, especially if it's not what I said."

When they hung up, Jessie decided to try his fishing luck one more time. He got a couple real good strikes but no real bites except for small ones. His rod and reel were put to rest, at least for this session.

Jessie went back to the house and took a private tour around the place. The bedroom he was to stay in had a bed, dresser and twenty-one inch TV. Shooter's clothes were in the dresser and closet. Only the bedroom, kitchen and front room were furnished. The basement was clean except for the table, chairs and surveillance equipment. The one thing he forgot was the alarm system in the front room. This meant that there had to be a bagman that picked up the money that was dropped off here, unless Shooter made deliveries. If he did the drops, who was watching the place while he was gone? He decided that the next time he and Chico made a drop, he would come back and stake out the place. Whoever came, he might find out where they split up the money.

Somehow, this whole thing didn't smell right. What if the five bosses all worked for one man who took care of dividing the loot? That person could be the brains behind getting them together. Each of the five could run their own territory, and the meetings held only to work out problems that came up. Yep, follow the money and see where it leads.

Between sleep, eating and fishing, the next twenty hours seemed to drag by. Jessie was glad when he saw Shooter coming back. In only a few hours, he would be holding Francine.

First thing Shooter asked when he got out of his car was "How many fish did you get?" "Nothing over eight inches so I was thinking that live bait and a boat out in deeper water might work. Any chance I could come out some evening and give it another try?"

Shooter said, "Any night but Thursdays…that's my TV night."

"OK, I'll give you a call if you have a phone."

"Call my cell. That's all we have here until they get some new lines run. But hell, any night but Thursday."

"Sounds great! Now all I have to do is find a bait store so I'll see you soon. Got to get ready for my date."

Thanks for watching the place for me and remember, don't mention that name."

"I have already forgotten what it was. You take it easy Shooter. Be seein' ya."

Chapter 24

Isn't it funny how your foot gets heavy when you're going to see someone you love? Jessie looked down at his speedometer and was thankful no police were around.

Despite his anxiety about seeing Francine again, his mind turned to other things. He would come back Thursday night to see who made the pickup, which could add to his job because he felt the underbosses were now ready for him to take out—and there could still be at least one left. Another thought came to his mind. What if this was a test to see how gangs could work together. It could be the start of a new wave of controlling large areas. With no wars, a lot of money would be saved. One gang of thugs could handle a large area to keep people in line which would be another large saving as you wouldn't need as many soldiers. Then in time, you could cut more overhead by less underbosses. Now this could be a sweet deal if handled right. Somebody put a lot of planning into this and what if he had help? Damn, this could be a lot bigger than anyone imagined.

Once he got home, he decided on a quick shower and shave. He then checked the phonebook for supper clubs and found one with reservations only. His luck was running with him as they had a couple openings so he made reservations for eight o'clock, which gave them ample time to get there. He left shortly after six to go to Francine's place but ran into Lee who was coming to see him.

"Hello Jessie, you got a FedEx today so thought it might be important."

"It sure is. I forgot it was coming. Had my mind on that girl from the restaurant."

"That would make most men forget just about anything. Anyway, you got it now, and I see you're going out so I'll let you go. Have fun and tell her hello from us."

"I'll do that and thanks for the mail."

Jessie drove to a park on his way and stopped to look at his pictures. With them blown up, the images were very clear. On the bottom of each picture was the person's name. On the back was the address and history of what was known about them. This was one group the town would be better off without.

First he put the pictures in his glove compartment and locked it but thought better of that. If a car was broken into, a locked compartment would seem to be a place for valuables. He decided to put them under his floor mat and could only hope they would be safe there.

He was finally on his way to Francine's place. When he approached the door, Francine once again opened it for him.

"May I say how beautiful you look?"

"Yes sir, you may and I thank you for saying it. You also look mighty nice." Before he could respond, her mother came in and said, "You make a fine looking couple, so kiss her hello and you can be on your way."

"Thank you Mama, but what if he doesn't want to kiss me?" Taking hold of her Jessie said, "Oh the things a man has to do" and before Francine could answer, Jessie kissed her. Stepping back but still holding her hands, all three laughed and any tension that might have existed was now gone.

"Now you kids go on and have a good time," Mama said.

On the way to the car Francine asked, "Where are we going tonight?"

"To Carlos Ray's Supper Club. I made reservations for eight o'clock. Do you approve?"

"That's a place I've heard is very good. Although I've never been there, but I'm willing to try it if you are."

"Good, but what if I asked you to go fishing, would you go?"

"I've never been fishing, but I guess it could be fun."

"Okay, how about living close to the ocean; would you be OK with that?" Jessie asked.

"Of course, I like the ocean but why are you asking?"

"I'm just trying to get to know you, which includes your likes and dislikes. Aren't you curious about what I like?"

"Well, that would be a yes and a no. Curiosity killed the cat. OK, how about the size of a family. Do you want lots of kids?"

"That would depend on what my wife wanted. After all, she has to bear them. I'd be happy for any, as long as they were healthy."

"What if she doesn't want any? Would that make a difference?"

"Do you mean would I love her less? No way. When I marry, my love will remain the same."

"Your answer is one most woman would like to hear," Francine said. "Too often men are set on what they want."

"I'm glad you like my answer and now the last question. What about the wedding ceremony?"

"Most woman dream about a large wedding from the time they're a small girls. At one time I was the same, but now it really doesn't matter. Mom and dad ran off when they tied the knot and still act like they're on their honeymoon. I hope my answers meet with your approval."

"I apologize for being so nosey. The trouble with me is I want to know all about you so I don't mess up. Your dad said you could get mean, and I was scared!" as he laughed.

"That sounds like dad. He tells me to ask the rowdy customers to leave. Of course he has a shotgun behind the bar so I'm not worried."

"You know I'm just teasing you about your dad."

"Yes, I know you are because if there was any real danger, he would take care of it himself. Everyone knows he is a Uterio."

Just then they rounded a curve in the road and saw the neon sign that read, "Carlos Ray's Supper Club."

"This looks like quite a place, and that parking lot looks full," Jessie said.

"From what I've heard, the food is excellent, but the prices are a little high. I guess that keeps out the troublemakers, but they also have a couple bouncers."

Jessie decided on valet service, and once out of the car, they entered into a dimly lit entry. They were met by the maître d' who asked his name before showing them to their table near the dance floor. After the waitress took their drink order, the band was playing a nice slow song so he asked Francine to dance.

When he took her into his arms, he told her that this was what he was looking forward to. There is nothing like a good slow dance to hold someone close and get to know them.

"What did they do when they couldn't dance?" Francine asked.

"Well, I would guess that once they kissed goodnight, it felt good so they just kept doing it."

"Then when we kissed goodnight, it didn't feel good?" she asked.

"Oh no Francine," Jessie said. "I liked it so much; I wanted it to last forever. I have never wanted to hold anyone as much as I want to hold you."

By the end of the first dance, it was obvious that she enjoyed being held as much as he enjoyed holding her. They returned to their table ordered steak dinners. While they waited for their dinner, they talked about so many things—like places to live and things they would do if they lived there. Francine told Jessie that her parents and her aunt and uncle on her mom's side were trying to sell their businesses. They both had people interested. Her dad was even talking of a warm climate.

"Does that mean you would consider an offer you might be getting soon?"

"Only if it came from the heart of the person asking," she said.

Before Jessie could say anything more, their food arrived.

The rest of the evening was a dream for both of them as they ate and talked. They were so comfortable with each other that spans of time went by with no conversation at all.

When they returned to her home, Jessie said, "Francine, I love you so much. I'm going to ask your dad's permission for your hand in marriage. I would like both your dad and mom's approval because I'm old fashioned and want them to like me. There is no way you don't know how I feel about you. I hope you feel the same towards me.

"My love for you grows more each day," Francine said. "I wasn't sure until the night we went to the show. Mom told me that you and I looked like we were made for each other. She was right; I fell in love with you that night. With the question you have just asked, I know, without a doubt, that you are the one for me."

"Francine, I'd like to come over on Monday night to speak to your folks. Do you think that would be OK and will they be home?"

"I'll make sure they're home and can't wait to see the look on my dad's face when you ask him," she responded.

Once again, their lips met as they sat on the porch swing. As they broke apart, Jessie told her that this was the ending of a beautiful night. Soon, there would not be an ending where he had to go home, as they would be one in body and spirit. He said he would have to leave now, as he didn't want to spoil that most beautiful evening.

"Darling, I'll see you Monday night. Until then, sleep tight. You and your mom can decide when and where. I'd like some time next month, but if that's too soon, I'll be happy whenever you choose." One last kiss and he was on his way. He didn't want to leave her but common sense said he'd better. Each kiss was becoming more intense and passionate.

Chapter 25

The more he thought about what happened to Jumbo, the more he realized the whole thing smelled bad. Tomorrow he would call Chico to see if he found out anything. What a shame about Jumbo and his girl. This was like a planned hit, but why? At that hour of the night, bars didn't keep much cash on hand. A couple hundred dollars wouldn't be worth two or possibly three murders. He thought that perhaps Thursday night might give him an answer. Perhaps the brain of this organization was going to put his men in critical places. Pure speculation wasn't answering anything so patience was all he really needed now.

He reached under his seat, took out the envelope with the pictures, and carried them into his place. Once he settled in with a cold beer, he decided to study them real close.

These were a real bunch of misfits. The brothers had a legitimate business that was run by someone else. They were the main suspects in the Gulardi killings and also had a payroll big enough to stay in good stead with the law. There was other paperwork included with the pictures that turned out to be a list of public officials. There were question marks beside three with a note that read, "these we're not sure of so when you know your timetable, call."

For the rest of the night, he committed everything to memory and then destroyed all the contents of the package.

He slept a little later Sunday morning but once awake, decided to go to Tony's bar. The crowd that was already outside the bar didn't surprise him. He went in and saw Chico was sitting with two guys at the back. Chico motioned for Jessie to join them. As Jessie approached the table, he realized that one of them was the same one who ran the enforcement crew.

"Jessie, you remember Scott, and this is Romero." Jessie shook hands with them both and sat down.

"Romero is from the East Side where we'll be going more often, and he'll tell us what we need to do," Chico said.

"No problem to me. As long as the money stays good, I'm his man," Jessie said.

With that, Chico added, "This is the one I was telling you about. Cool as ice when trouble comes along, and he's not just your average guy. He thinks before he moves."

"Can he handle pickups and deliveries alone yet?" Romero asked.

"One more trip and no doubt. He still needs to meet a couple more people first," Chico replied.

"Good, on Tuesday, hit both places and get him ready to fly solo. I'll call you if there are any changes in the plans. Oh, one more thing. Thursday will be the same route. Can he handle that?"

"Yes, we went in together so he could meet Tony, Clyde and Girt, so they know him."

"OK, you go with him Tuesday and meet the boat; then he can go Thursday by himself. I have another job for you starting Thursday. We'll get together at Leo's on Wednesday to discuss it. We've got to go, but we'll see you soon."

When Romero and Scott left, Jessie ordered another cup of coffee and said, "Looks like they replaced Jumbo with Romero and you, with me. So who are you replacing?"

"That is the question," Chico replied. "And it's a good question. I'll find out Thursday."

"Yeah, but go see Leo? Who did Jumbo take his orders from? Maybe Leo has been his boss all along."

"That's possible. It could be, but he never said. All he ever got were phone calls whenever I was with him. Hell, he was here almost all the time, except on Thursday nights when he went bowling. That might be when he met the boss."

"How much money did those robbers get from here, do you know?"

"Not much. You know underneath the drawer in the cash register, they missed a couple big bills. Must have been in a hell of a hurry to get out of here. On top of that, they left a Rolodex watch on Jumbo's wrist."

"Sounds like a couple of dumb ass robbers or a professional hit on Jumbo."

"What do you mean by a hit on Jumbo?"

"Nothing really, but no one from here is stupid enough to rob this place—so one of two things happened. Dumb ass robbers or good hit."

"Yeah, I see what you mean. Could be either one."

"While you think about it, I've got a few things to do. I'll pick you up at six a.m. on Tuesday unless you call."

* * * * *

Once on the road, Jessie drove from memory to the addresses of all the bosses to keep it fresh in his mind. All five had homes on the outskirts of town. Only the brothers were located close to the businesses. As he was passing through both towns, he noticed a couple jewelry stores and decided to make a couple stops there tomorrow. He could buy an engagement ring for Francine with the understanding that she could exchange it if she wanted something different. He would have brought her with him to pick out her own; but this way, he would have a ring to put on her finger at the time of his formal proposal. If he made it real special, maybe she wouldn't want to exchange it. Monday was getting close, and he wanted this job done before marrying her so she would never find out that he was involved.

Chapter 26

He hoped that Thursday would give an answer to his many questions. He ran the questions through his mind, yet again. Who were the brains behind this new way to run a territory? Who split up the money and where? Did each boss run one part of the operation like the numbers—one drop, one call house, etc? This would be a lot smarter because each boss would only have to answer for one phase of the operation. He would get a better idea at the next meeting by listening to them with his bug.

He was sure of one thing. This would be his last guard job. If they weren't all there, a sniper rifle would be used. He decided to cook at home tonight so he could catch up on some paperwork. Letter writing was not his forte', but he had to get the names down to send to his contact. When he left here, there should be a large cleanup job for the authorities. Next, he took his small camera and installed it in his belt buckle so he could get some pictures to send. The schooner they would be meeting again had to have a contact for getting those drugs. The warehouse should be staked out before they busted it. All the other joints could be taken down, although they would just set up someplace else.

Maybe, what he was doing would save some people from a life of hell. Soon, someone else could worry about it, but already he was thinking how to get all the bosses together again. Once he knew the answers to his questions, the contact would be told. His job was almost over. How it was done, no one would ever be told. There wouldn't be any proof how he set it off but rather that he was just outside and could have been killed. When the blast went off, the police would get some calls from the neighbors. They would be there within five minutes. He wanted to be sure he was gone because there would be a lot of questions he didn't want to answer.

He could park his car in an area where falling debris wouldn't block his exit. The detonator and listening device could be thrown into the deep part of the lake where they wouldn't be found. The transmitter for the listening device would probably be found, but there weren't any prints on that so he was still safe. The only issue to be taken care of was the plates on his car. Some nosey neighbor could write it down so a roll of duct tape would solve that problem. Chico was the only link to him and Francine—and the only way to find him was through her family. There was really no choice in the matter; he had to go. With Jumbo already dead, no one else knew about him.

Tuesday evening he would take a ride out to see Shooter and perhaps do a little fishing. Maybe he could pick Shooter's brain and look for a good place to park. On his way back, he could check time and mileage and see how long it took him to turn off the main road in the event someone else was coming his way. Everything was so odd. When Joe was killed, they had a meeting, and he was only a soldier. When Jumbo was killed, it was like no one cared. Something just didn't smell right.

What if they put a hit on, with no reason to talk about it, because it was made to look like some dumb ass robber? But, how did they pick his replacement so fast, unless they had already replaced him? Romero sure came in quick and knew what jobs he and Chico had to do. How did he know that? Why was Scott, the Enforcer, with him? Was he making sure his men were clean? Only the bartender could identify who did the shooting. Because he was in a coma, was he being allowed to stay alive. The last thing that made it look like a hit was the fact that it was the bartender's first day on the job. Tony had left the new man there by himself.

Maybe it was all part of a bigger plan to streamline the organization. One thing for sure, when it came time to cut the overhead, he would be helping them out a lot.

Jessie kicked back with a cold beer to watch the news, then a movie before he went to bed.

In the morning he went to Mom and Pop's for some breakfast. He was surprised that Francine wasn't there so he asked her aunt where she was.

"She's on the later shift on Mondays and besides, we hear somebody has an important question to ask her parents tonight. Is there any truth in that?"

Jessie laughed and said it was a good possibility, then added, "I do have a little problem with all this. I don't know her ring size. Would you happen to know?

"She wears a slightly larger size than I do so why don't you get her a size seven because my 6 ½ is a little tight for her."

"Thanks for letting me know. Wish me luck, OK? I'll probably need it."

Jessie drove to one of the jewelry stores he had seen and went in to look for a ring he thought his Francine would like. The clerk showed him many, but he finally decided on a beautiful half karat, princess cut that he thought suited her best. He paid, and with the ring box in his pocket, he headed for the hardware store where he purchased a roll of duct tape. Once his shopping was done, he drove to Tony's Bar to see if Chico was there. He drove all around the building, but there was no sign of Chico's car so he decided to call him on his cell phone.

When Chico answered, Jessie said, "Hi Chico, where the hell are you?"

"I'm about a mile from Tony's," Chico said. "How about you?"

Jessie said, "Sitting in the parking lot getting ready to go in."

"OK, order me a coffee, and I'll be right there."

Jessie stepped through the back door. As he did, he noticed only one couple sitting at the bar. Tony, himself, was serving drinks. An older woman walked toward him to take his order. She asked him what he wanted, and he ordered two cups of coffee saying, "The other guy will be here in a minute." As she set the cups on the table, Jessie saw Chico pull up.

He came in and sat down.

"What are you doing out so early?"

"I had a couple stops to make and wondered if you would be here so I drove over. Have there been any changes since the last time we talked?"

"No, tomorrow we go to the boat and warehouse and then to the drop-off. Once that's done, you're on your own."

"How about you Chico? You're not leaving this area, are you?"

"No, I don't think so. I'll find out my new job Tuesday night when we come back. Check your pay on Friday. There should be a raise as you're starting on your own. That's what they did when

I came along."

"How about their next meeting? Are we still the guards now that you're on another job?"

"I know you will be, but I don't know about me. Doesn't matter. Its easy duty. With all the changes going on, they could do anything they want. After all, you only work two days a week, the same as I did before. Anyway, I'll know soon. My advice to you is to keep your nose clean."

"Don't worry about me Chico. You're the one going into uncharted waters. You want another cup before I leave?"

"Hell no, I piss more with coffee than I do with beer. You go ahead; just pick me up tomorrow. See you then and don't be late."

With time on his hands, Jessie drove to the three places scheduled for the pick-ups on Thursday. It looked like business was good. He jotted down the addresses of each place and drove back to Mom and Pop's.

When he got inside, Francine's mom came toward him so he decided to show her the ring. He said, "Please try it on so I can see how it looks on a lady's hand."

"Oh no, it's too pretty, but if you don't mind, I'd like to show it to dad."

"Please do; I just hope Francine will like it."

"Jessie, it is perfect, and Francine will love it." When she returned from the kitchen, she told Jessie that dad thought it was perfect also.

Jessie felt much better knowing that Francine's folks had approved of his choice and felt she would be happy with it too. He headed home not only to get ready for his proposal tonight, but also to go over plans on where they would begin their lives together. He was hoping they could be married within the month, but he wasn't sure she would want a wedding that fast.

Chapter 27

Jessie was deep in thought when his cell phone rang and it was his contact. "I wanted you to know that our man in New York said there's a rumor that someone from here is going to be out your way for a parlay regarding a trade of some kind. We don't know what it's about, but they're setting up a meeting soon. Any news on your end?"

"I'm hoping that after the next meeting I'll be telling you both goodbye 'cause I'll be long gone. I'll be sending you a list and whatever pictures I can get. Then the real work will start for you guys. I hope you have plenty of help; otherwise, you're going to lose a lot if you don't hit a bunch of them at a time. Once they hear of a few, the rest will take off."

"We figure to hit only the big ones because the small fish can be handled by the local police. The dope is what we consider the most dangerous; the rest on a more local basis. When you leave, remember the number in case you ever need another job. I'll wish you the best of luck now, and unless you call, we won't be in touch anymore."

"Thanks, I might need some luck before I'm done. You guys be good and luck to you too. Goodbye."

* * * * *

Jessie started getting ready for tonight. After a hot shower and shave, he dressed in a sports jacket and slacks. Once he felt everything was just right, he decided that he was now ready to go see Francine.

He was a little early so he decided to stop by Sal's Bar to get a cold drink and wondered if perhaps Francine was still at work. When he went through the door, he saw her dad behind the bar, walked over and said, "How about me buying you a drink?"

"No way, on this night, I'm treating," Sal said. "My girl is walking on air. I've sold the restaurant and will be a retired man next week, so it's my treat all the way. Francine went home as soon as I signed the papers because she wanted to tell Mom, but I know she wanted to get ready for tonight."

Through the conversation and excitement of the unfolding events, both men had finished their drinks and Sal said, "Maybe we could have one more before we leave, then hightail it home before the ladies get mad. I hope you brought a good appetite as Mom's going to feed you. She thinks that since you're in your own place now, you must not be getting enough to eat."

"The thought of food hasn't entered my mind all day. Actually, I've been a little nervous 'cause I've never done this before."

"Just relax Son, there ain't nothing to it. All the real work comes later."

"Thanks Pop, now I'm really worried."

Jessie was getting ready to leave and Sal said, "Tell them I'll be right home as soon as I get my night man straight."

The drive to Francine's place took only a few minutes. Jessie found himself on her porch, and the door opened. Francine was in his arms greeting him with a welcoming kiss. As they parted, he told her how beautiful she looked. Her eyes were sparkling, and her cheeks were somewhat flushed as she thanked him for the compliment.

"I hope you're as hungry as Mom thinks you are. Dad will be home soon we hope."

"When I left him, he was getting ready to leave. We had a drink together to celebrate the sale of the restaurant. Mom must be happy to know it's sold."

"She's on cloud nine and already looking at brochures from Florida and California. Dad told me they'll be moving, but he's not sure where. He said they would probably take a vacation and look around real good before making a final decision. According to him, this will be their last move so he wants it to be a good one. Mom's hoping her sister and her husband will move to wherever they settle down. Did you say anything to Dad yet?"

"No, not yet but I'm sure he knows already. I think when he gets home and settles down, I'll ask him and all you have to do is have Mom there too."

No sooner had the words left Jessie's lips when Pop opened up the porch screen, saw Francine, and asked, "How did Mom take the news?"

"Like a duck to water," Francine said. "She's already looking for a place in the sun."

"Francine, honey, will you please bring wine so we can all have a drink before dinner?"

As the two men sat down in the living room, Francine returned with the four glasses of wine and her mother as well. Once everyone was seated, Jessie began speaking.

"Pop, by now, you and Mom know how I feel about Francine. I love her with all my heart, and tonight, with permission from you both, I'd like to ask her to marry me."

"Son," Pop said, "We're glad you were man enough to ask us, and by all means, you have our permission to marry our daughter; that is of course, if she agrees."

Jessie turned toward Francine, dropped to one knee and produced the ring box, opened it and said, "Francine, will you marry me?"

She took the ring out of the box and handed it to Jessie and said "Yes Jessie, I'll marry you." Jessie placed the ring on her finger, and as he did so, she started to cry tears of joy. He gently took her in his arms and kissed her in a most loving and tender way.

With that, Pop cleared his throat.

"Well Dad, I think we can relax and go eat. When you kids get ready, we'll be at the table waiting for you. Ha-ha".

Once Francine's folks had left the room, Jessie had to have one more kiss. This one was all he needed to know that she was his completely.

They walked into the dining room. Once they were all seated at the table, Pop said the blessing for the food and then asked Jessie what their plans were once they were married.

"Well pop, that will be up to my new wife. When my parents died, they left me well off, money-wise, so we can live wherever she chooses, here or abroad. All my business should be finished within a couple weeks so I'll let her and Mom pick a good day for the wedding."

Pop said, "Knowing them, they've probably got it picked out already."

"No we have not," Mom said. "Your daughter wants to be married like we were. How and when is up to them to decide, and I can only hope they invite us."

At that, Francine jumped into the conversation and said, "Mom, you know we will. Who else would ask you and Dad if he could date me and if he could marry me? You know you both will be there."

"Mom," Jessie said, "once we decide where and when it's to be—whether Vegas, London, or wherever—you and Dad will go with us. You are the only family I have since both my real and adoptive parents are all dead. I can only hope that when Francine and I are married, you will be able to accept me as a son."

Before Jessie could move, Mom had her arms around his neck and said, "We did that when Francine started talking about you. We both felt you two were meant for each other for many reasons; but one that showed was that no one has ever given her a desire to dress up. She has always been a strong-willed girl. It's been her way or the highway. Love is a strange thing."

Jessie said, "Mom, that's what I thought. Now I have trouble getting to sleep. All I can think of is her. I want to hold her so tight, but I'm scared of hurting her; and although I know she's not that fragile, I still wonder."

"Son, I felt the same way when I married her Mom," Pop said, "But come to find out, they're stronger than us in many ways. Besides, she's my bouncer and can be mean as hell. Ha-ha."

"Thanks a lot Dad," Francine said. "You'll scare him off. Oh well, maybe in a few years I'll meet someone, but until then, you and Mom can take care of me."

"No, no! Jessie knows I'm just fooling around," Pop said. "You are as delicate as a flower."

"That's OK Pop," Jessie said, "I'll take her on a trial basis for a few years." With that, they all laughed and although unspoken, there was a sense within them all that this was indeed, family.

After dinner, Jessie and Francine went out to the porch swing. She had her head on his shoulder. He asked her if she and Mom had discussed the wedding ceremony.

"Yes," Francine said, "We thought that in a couple weeks we could all go to Las Vegas. The folks could look over the area, and if you like the idea, we could get married there."

"Like it"! Jessie said, "I love it! All my other business should be finished by then and after that, I'm all yours."

Francine was beaming and said, "Pop signed the papers today

and has to stay for ten days to get the new owners acquainted with the operation of the business; then anytime after that, we're free."

"Dearest Francine, why don't you take this next week to decide where you'd like to settle after we're married. I've got to finish my work here and will also have to take a couple overnight trips but I should be back by Saturday. We can go out for dinner and a show then, if you want."

"Now that the business has been sold and I'm home, you can call me more often; at least I can talk to you. If you finish with your business early, call me because even though you haven't left yet, I miss you already and more than you know."

"Darling, that works two ways. Holding you is all I dream of. I want you beside me day and night. Once my job is completed here, we'll be together all the time." With that, Jessie pulled Francine into his arms. They shared deep, passionate kisses, which made restraint nearly impossible.

Jessie pulled away and told Francine how much he loved her and despite their brewing passion, said he had to leave in order to begin his forthcoming trip early. Francine walked out with him to his car. After several more loving kisses, Jessie forced himself to drive away.

Chapter 28

Jessie now had to get himself into the mental state that would be required to continue and hopefully complete his mission.

Tomorrow he'd go get a load of dope with Chico and deliver them to the same places as before. Thursday, he'd be a pickup man and take the money to Shooter. Tuesday he'd watch the meeting place and do a mental inventory of the people that showed up. Once Friday came, he'd see about making a meeting happen which might include taking out one of the bosses. He was sure that would do the trick. If no meeting was called on that one hit, he might have to take out another. Taking them all out in one place was the best because there was less chance of something going wrong; but he would take them out—one way or the other and soon. With the plan pretty well fixed in his mind, Jessie went to bed and slept well.

Once Jessie awoke, he drove to the 7-11 and picked up two cups of coffee and donuts. Chico was standing at the curb when he pulled up to the usual place.

"Fresh coffee and donuts for us both Chico, and since I bought breakfast, you can buy lunch."

"OK, that's settled, we can eat lunch at that Crab Shack down by the docks before we drive back."

"Speaking of the dock, Chico, we never see a cop down there, only an occasional highway patrol on the road. Do you know something I don't?"

"When you grease the right wheel, it doesn't squeak, the same with a palm. No patrols in that area when we're there. See what you can do when you know who to grease? Funny thing is it doesn't have to be someone real big like down town."

"So the only one we need to look out for is the State Patrol? Good, I was a little worried with that much junk on us going back."

"Our outfit has a lot of clout Jessie. Hell, they checked you out in a few days, and that's why you're still here.

"When we get to the warehouse, drive around to the back, and we'll both go in. Today's load is a hell of a lot of Mary Jane or Pot, whatever you call it. All the good stuff comes in by boat, and then they store it here. The white stuff that we get at the docks also comes in, but they don't store it 'cause it's too much money'. I think they deliver one suitcase at a time in various places up and down the coast."

"I don't know if you've got to pee but between the coffee and the drive, I've got to stop at the next place," Jessie said.

"Go ahead," Chico said, "and I'll get us another coffee while you go."

The bathroom stop was just an excuse for Jessie, as he didn't have to pee that bad but wanted to check out his camera. Today he hoped to get some good pictures to send when his job was over. Satisfied that everything was working well, he returned to the car where Chico had them both a coffee.

"Boy, do I feel better. Didn't think I'd ever stop. Thanks for the coffee Chico; at least now I've got room to hold it. Did you get any news on your new job yet?"

"No, I've got to meet Romero Thursday, and he's going to go with me. I did hear they may be meeting this weekend 'cause some strange guy's supposed to be there. That means me and you work, unless they change me for someone else. One more thing, half our load of Pot goes to Leo's. His crew will meet us there after we take the Coke to the plant."

"When you say Leo's, do you mean his home or the Carry Inn?" Jessie asked.

"At the Inn or should I say behind the Inn. There's a house back there with a garage, and they use that as a pickup point for their "sales people." And he laughed. "After we leave the warehouse, we'll have lunch, and then go to the schooner."

When they arrived at the warehouse, Jessie backed in at the loading dock at the rear of the building. They went in to see a man by the name of "Salis." Jessie looked around and saw trucks being unloaded and pallets of food, drinks, cigarettes, and dog food being stored.

"Salis," Chico said, "I want you to meet Jessie and we need four bags of fertilizer for the car in the back. Jessie will come down and see you next time."

Salis called to one of his workers who was driving a forklift. The man drove directly to a pallet on which were four large bags of dog food and moved them to the back loading dock. Jessie followed him out and loaded them into the trunk of his car. As Jessie walked back, he snapped a few pictures, including a couple of Salis.

Once they were back in the car, Jessie said, "Boy Chico, that's a slick way to transport those goods. Does everybody in there know the score?"

"Are you kidding? From what I hear, only Salis knows. That way, if there's a leak, only one is held accountable. Whoever got us all together believes the fewer that know, the better. There is one badass crew that takes care of trouble all over, and no one wants to see them coming to visit. It used to take three and four men to do what we do alone so it cuts the overhead. He'll have the organization streamlined in a couple more months."

"You know Chico, if this guy is so good and things are starting to run so smooth, why does he need all those bosses?"

"Each boss controls one section until everyone works as one unit when and where they're needed. In time, they may spread to other places and do the same there as here. That's why the other guy is coming to see how well they work together. Now, let's go eat. I'm not only hungry, but I'm hungry for some seafood."

After eating at the Crab Shack, they drove to the slip that held the "Tiki," the name of the schooner. This time when Jessie parked the car, they both went on board.

"Hello Mon, glad you got here before I leave."

"Come on Fero," said Chico, "we're not late. We had to stop and eat because they don't have any place by us that serves food like we get here. Look who I've brought for you to meet. This is Jessie, and he's the one who'll be taking my place."

"Glad to meet you Jessie. Now I go below and get your merchandise."

Jessie acted like he was doing a little sightseeing around the schooner. Once back by the stern, he snapped a couple pictures including one of Fero as he came up the stairs. Jessie and Chico each grabbed one of the very large suitcases and walked back down to the car. As Jessie reached the car, he turned around toward the schooner and saw the crew weighing anchor as they prepared to get under way.

As Jessie put the suitcases into the backseat, he said, "That Jamaican was ready to go so it's a good thing we got here when we did."

"No sweat kid," Chico said, he don't go nowhere 'till we get here. No delivery, no money, simple as that. What say we head home?"

"Any stops before we get to the factory?"

"No, head there and we'll drop off these cases. Then to the Carry Inn, and we're through for today and tomorrow".

"Do those two brothers still work at the business?" Jessie asked.

"No Jessie," said Chico, "the amusement end of the business is run by the stockholders. Romero told me that this is the last shipment to be delivered here which is probably just another change to streamline production."

"Maybe that's what they got in mind for you Chico, someone has to run it."

"Jessie," Chico said, "I'm afraid that isn't the case. The guy you saw today is the best in the business. He has only one helper to get it cut up and bundled into smaller packages."

"Then I don't know it gets out," Jessie said.

"Maybe someday you'll find out. Anyway, we're here."

Jessie drove through the gate, past the factory, and around to the small building nestled unobtrusively in the rear portion of the yard. As they got out, each lifted one of the suitcases out of the car. Chico led the way to a rear door, which he quickly opened without knocking. As they entered the room, the two guys sitting at a table playing cards looked up. The older of the two said, "Hi Chico, see you made it again."

"This is the last trip for me. I've brought you the new man. Jessie, meet Larry and Tom, with Larry being your main contact here." They shook hands all around and then Chico said, "Have you heard that they may move you to some other place?"

"I'm to be packed up by next Monday and ready to go, but no one has said where to yet," Larry said. "Hey, you guys want a cold beer before you leave?"

Chico was ready for a cool one and said, "That sounds fine for me. How about you Jessie?"

"Yeah, I could go for a cool one. Since I'm the closest one to the fridge, I'll even get them for us." His offer to get the four beers gave Jessie the opportunity to get a picture of Larry and Tom. There was a minimum of conversation while the four drank, and soon the beer cans were empty. It was time to leave and said their goodbye. Once back in the car, Chico instructed Jessie to head for the Inn.

When they arrived, Chico said, "Drive around to the garage. We'll put the dog food in there."

Jessie parked and walked to the rear of the car and opened the trunk. At the same time, Chico used a key to open the door and then removed it from his key ring and gave it to Jessie. Without talking, they both worked to move the dog food into the garage.

"Pull the car up to the Inn so we can go in to see Leo," Chico said.

Jessie did as he was directed, and they were soon going by the pool tables toward the back room. Chico knocked on the door and someone said "Enter."

They walked in and saw Leo sitting behind a huge desk. The two huge guys sitting on each side of the room stood up as they entered.

"Hello Chico," Leo said, "Looks like you brought a helper with you."

"Sure did Leo. We wanted you to know that the dog food has arrived," Chico said. "You remember Jessie, don't you?"

"He's a hard one to forget. I heard he's taking your place. That's good; maybe I'll see him more often."

Jessie couldn't help but smile a little and said, "Nice to see you again, and I hope everything is going smooth."

"Now that's what I like to hear...Smooth, not simply good," Leo said. "He's not only tough, but he has a brain that works too. I'll remember that. Keep up the good work Jessie. It could pay off big time for you. Now you boys go have a couple drinks on me."

While they were sitting at the table with their drinks, Chico said, "Where in the world did you come up with 'smooth'? Damn, I wish I'd said that. Looks to me like Leo likes the way you act. Who knows, maybe you'll move up the ladder faster than others have."

"Hell, Leo's the only boss I've met. What do the others do? Have they got clubs or do any work or have jobs?"

"No, they don't work per se. One owns Tony's but never comes around. The two brothers draw salaries from their once-owned business. Sharpo still travels a little but what he does, who knows. Leo is the young one and a college boy from the Midwest. He bought out the owner of the Carry Inn about six months ago and has done real well there. Those two gorillas in there are guys he brought with him. They arrived a few days after Leo, along with a few of those bikers. Next thing you know, he had a steady stream of traffic."

"Sounds like a good organizer who knows how to get things

done. Let me know when your ready to cutout."

"How about now?" Chico said. "I got someone to go see so tonight you can drop me off at my pad."

"No problem," Jessie said. "When we get to Tony's, tell me where to go."

"Go straight by Tony's, then three blocks to the right. It's the end house on the right."

"You and your wife live there?" Jessie asked.

"No wife, a part-time girlfriend...and tonight we're going to celebrate my new job. When I hear about the meeting, I'll give you a call."

Chapter 29

After dropping Chico off, Jessie stove to a store and bought a six-pack to take with him to his stakeout. Tonight he would stay until ten o'clock. If there wasn't any luck, he would do the same each night for a few days.

Jessie found a place to watch the gate unobserved. While he waited, he called Francine and told her he wouldn't be back for a few more days but would call at least once each day until he was home.

Francine hesitantly said, "Jessie, honey, do you remember I told you I had two uncles, my dad's brothers? Well, they were killed today in a boating accident."

"Do you know what happened?" Jessie asked.

"Yes," she said, "The boat they were on was anchored out in the harbor, and they decided to stay all night in order to fish today. A short circuit down by the motor evidently started a fire. Since they were asleep, they just never woke up."

"Honey, I'm so sorry. I know this must be very hard on your Dad," Jessie said.

"Not really. Dad said they would die before anyone else did. If anyone deserved death, it was them. He was sorry that they were of the same name because of the shame they put on it. Dad said that leaving here now is easier than before. Mom said to tell you hello and to hurry home."

"I may get back Friday the way things are going—at least I hope so."

They talked for about twenty minutes about being together, along with the up-coming wedding, and after a few "I love you" hung up.

* * * * *

Jessie couldn't help but think about what Francine had said about the accident. It certainly made him wonder. With the two bosses gone, the field was really narrowed down—and taking out those two hadn't been all that difficult. A drugged glass of wine or food, then start the fire after messing up some wiring, and "Poof," two high-overhead personnel gone. Either way it went, Jessie felt relieved because he wasn't responsible for the deaths of Francine's uncles. He wondered what she would think if she knew what his line of work was.

Around 10 p.m., Jessie decided to call it a night as no one had come in or gone out. He decided that tomorrow he would start early and finish his pick-up. Once he did his drop, he could talk to Shooter for a little while, and then he'd watch the gate again.

When he got back home, he took the film out of his camera and installed the new roll for tomorrow. He put the used roll into the envelope that he'd mail before work tomorrow. His day was done so after a beer and warm shower, he turned in for the night and slept well.

In the morning, the first thing Jessie did was head for the FedEx office to mail his valuable film to his contact. He didn't want Francine to know he was in town so he decided to have breakfast at Tony's. He was on his second cup of coffee when Chico walked in and sat down across from Jessie in the booth.

"Looks like you got up early today to start your new job," Jessie said.

"Romero is going to call me here so we can meet," Chico said, "and it must be someplace I don't know or he could have told me."

"What about the two Uterio brothers killed in that boating accident?" Jessie said.

Chico's shock was evident and he said, "Where the hell did you get that from? I ain't heard nothing. When did this happen?"

"It was yesterday. Evidently they went on a fishing trip, and while they were asleep late at night, the boat caught fire. They didn't get out."

"Well, I'll say this," said Chico, "it couldn't have happened to nicer guys. Hell, even their own family won't lose any sleep because of it. Hey, Jessie, what are you doing out so early?"

"Oh, just thought I'd get done early, and maybe go over the

Jersey to do a little gambling tonight. Give me a call tomorrow, if you know anything about us working this weekend. Now I've got to cut out of here and get my work done. You take care. I hope you enjoy your new job. Let me know."

Jessie dropped money on the table for his breakfast and tip and drove to the bookie joint first. He saw Clyde and asked him how he was.

"Not bad, Jessie. It's been a good week, and the house has done real good. Anytime you get a convention in town, we get a lot of play. You been to see Girt yet?"

"No, Clyde," Jessie said, "I'm headed there next, and with all this crowd, she should have done alright too."

"I'll bet that Troy did good too as his place is within walking distance for them. They're probably like me. I'd rather walk than catch a cab; then I can leave whenever I want."

"Well, I hope next week is as good Clyde; see you then."

Jessie took the package that Clyde had given him and went to see Girt, the Madam at the Pleasure House. Her business had been extremely good. She gave him a bigger package than last week, and the same was true for Troy who also had a larger package for him.

Jessie finished his collection and drove to see Shooter. Once he arrived, he looked around to determine the best parking spot for the next meeting. When he made his decision, he parked in front of the house and knocked on the door.

Shooter answered the door and said, "Looks like you're the first one today."

"Yeah, just wondered if you heard about the brothers."

"Yes, I heard but the only surprise I had was that it took so long. They've been dead weight, along with a couple more, but you didn't hear that from me. Maybe that family you were asking about can finally rest in their graves."

"Has anybody talked about the meeting?" Jessie asked.

"No, only that we're looking for one before long so don't make any plans for this Friday or Saturday night because I'm not sure which one."

"OK," Jessie said, "and maybe we can fish one day next week? In any case, I'll pay you a visit and we'll see. Since I have tonight off, I think I'll drive over to Jersey and do a little gambling. Don't worry. I'll be back sometime tonight or early tomorrow so you take care, Shooter."

Jessie returned back the way he came and stopped to get

something to eat to take with him to his observation post. He watched for the next four hours. Only two men arrived about an hour apart, stayed only a short time and then left. Some time had passed when he saw a familiar car, Chico's. He was glad that his own car was well hidden. Chico was either making a delivery or a pickup as he didn't stay long. Jessie watched when Chico left and saw him locking the gate. If the gate was being locked, Chico must be the last visitor here for the night so Jessie decided to follow him.

Staying back far enough to remain undetected, Jessie followed Chico to a large home set back off the road and realized it was Leo's place. Once again, Chico stayed only a short while and then left, returning back the way the way he had come.

It was still too light for Jessie to go in and look over the house and surroundings. He drove to a restaurant and ate dinner, and by the time he had finished, darkness had set in. He returned to the area by Leo's place and parked down the road. Once he was confident that all was clear, he went over a small fence and made his way to the window and looked in. The room was dimly lit, but he could see Leo and some older man watching television like they didn't have a care in the world. At the end of the sofa, Jessie could see one of the large suitcases. Jessie checked around and was sure that no one else was there so he left and drove away.

As he drove, he was thinking about the situation. Leo was obviously the moneyman, but was he smart enough to be the brains? The answer would come soon enough.

Since he had told everyone he was going to Jersey to gamble, Jessie decided to drive to Atlantic City where he got a room for the night, just in case someone decided to do some checking. He left early the next morning and was soon walking into Tony's. There sitting at a back booth was Chico eating breakfast.

"Well, well, the gambler has returned," Chico, said, "so how much did you lose?"

"Not that much, only a couple hundred, but the food was good and the women hot," Jessie said.

"Your phone ain't broke, is it?" Chico asked.

"No, why?" Jessie asked.

"You could have stayed in Jersey tonight; the meeting is tomorrow night," Chico informed him.

"Damn, here I hurried home for no reason. Maybe I'll go back so I'll be there at six."

"Good," said Chico, "I'll see you then."

Chapter 30

With nothing else to do, Jessie went home to shower and kick back for a few. Once he had showered, shaved and dressed, he called Francine and asked her if she was free for the day.

Francine was excited to hear from him and said, "Yes my love, I'm free for the day. Mom was hoping you would be over so we can discuss the date you'll be free to go to Vegas. They put the house on the market today, and according to the realtor, it won't take long to sell."

"Tell your Mom I'm on my way and should be there in about thirty minutes. Does she need anything I can pick up at the store on my way?"

"No honey," Francine said, "we went to the store yesterday so please hurry and get here. I really miss you."

"OK doll," Jessie said, "I'll be there in no time. Bye for now."

True to his word and because his foot had been a little heavy on pedal, he was soon walking up the steps and into the arms of his Francine. When they finally stepped apart after a deep and passionate kiss, Jessie said, "Boy, next time I'll be gone for three days, but we'd better get married soon 'cause you sure make it tough for me."

Francine laughed and said, "I know, and it sure feels good!" They both laughed then, and Francine opened the door so they could enter the house. Mom was sitting on the couch watching TV and said, "Hello, Jessie, I hope everything is going all right with your business."

"Yes ma'am," Jessie said, "I'm hoping that by next week I'll be completely through. Doesn't Pop finish then too?"

"Next Friday will be his last day," Mom said, "and that's why we were wondering when would be a good day to leave."

"If I had my way, we would leave today, but since I can't, I can only promise that it will be very soon. I know Pop will agree that the final decision will be up to you ladies. I've got to leave again tomorrow, but I should be back by Sunday afternoon. Today I'd like to take you both to lunch with one stop on the way. In the meantime, and while you both get ready, any chance for this guy could get a glass of wine?"

"OK Mom," Francine said, "you heard what Jessie said. You go get ready while I get a drink for my man."

Once they were in the car, Jessie drove to a jewelry store and parked in front.

"Come on ladies, I need your help. I've never bought a wedding ring before so I'd like your help picking it out."

"Honey, the engagement ring you got me is so very beautiful, and to be quite honest, all I'd really like is a plain gold band. I'd like you to wear one too. We can have a double-ring ceremony with matching gold wedding bands if that's OK with you."

Jessie agreed and started to drive away when Mom said, "Did someone say something about eating? I'm starved!"

"You win, food it is. I passed a place called Carlo's Bistro so how does that sound? It's a fair drive from here, but I've heard the food is good." Everyone agreed, and the conversation continued with Jessie saying, "What about your Aunt and Uncle, Francine, have they sold out yet?"

"Yes, their house is sold," Francine said, "but the new owner doesn't take over until the first of the month so they'll be here to watch Mom and Dad's place until it's sold. Once my folks find the new town and place they want to live, they'll call my aunt and uncle to see if they want to move there too."

Jessie and the two women enjoyed a wonderful lunch and once they finished, Jessie said, "So, what would you like to do now?"

"Why don't we stay in tonight," Francine said, "and watch a movie on TV, eat dinner and then you and I can spend a little time on the porch swing. That way, when it gets time for you to leave, we'll already be there. We can have more time for kisses."

As it turned out, Francine was right. They all enjoyed some family time and before Jessie had to leave that night, Pop suggested that he'd like to leave the following Friday for Las Vegas, let the kids get married, and then decide where to start looking for a new place, perhaps someplace in Arizona.

"Why don't Francine and I leave two days earlier, get the blood test, a marriage license and arrange for a room for you and Mom. We can have the ceremony right after you and Mom land at the airport; that is, if she and Mom agree to this plan."

"Son, if you wanted to leave right this minute, she would be ready before you finished saying so!"

"Oh Dad," Francine said, "You know it would take me a little longer than that! But don't worry my darling Jessie, I'll be ready Wednesday morning if you tell me that's when we'll be leaving."

"Well then, it's settled," Jessie said, "I'll have everything ready Tuesday as all it takes is a phone call. I don't know when I'll be back—Sunday or Monday—but I know I'll be here sometime on Tuesday. Anyway, I'll call to keep you informed, my love."

Jessie didn't really want to leave, but after thanking Mom and Pop for dinner, he kissed Francine goodbye and said, "I'll call tomorrow honey, to update you on my timing." After numerous heartfelt kisses, Jessie forced himself to leave.

Chapter 31

As Jessie was lying in bed the following morning, he knew he'd have to keep his mind off of Francine for a couple days. Thoughts of her sometimes seemed to scramble his brain and made his heart seem to skip beats. He loved her so very much but knew he had to concentrate on his job and the task that was now nearing completion.

After showering and dressing, he drove to Tony's to eat some breakfast and meet with Chico. Much to his surprise, Chico wasn't there. While waiting for his food, he dialed Chico's cell phone. When Chico answered, Jessie said, "Hello you old Son, where you at?"

"Sleeping in," Chico said, "Mona wanted to mess around, what's up?"

"I was just thinking about going a little early and doing some fishing before they start. Then I'll already be there when they arrive."

"Why not," Chico said, "if that turns you on. They said be there no later than six thirty so just call Shooter and let him know that you're coming early."

"I'll do that now. See you when you get there and go ahead and have some fun while you can. By the way Chico, do you like your new job?"

"Piece of cake," Chico said, "as long as I forget what I do."

"Well then, have fun. Bye for now."

When Jessie hung up, he immediately called Shooter and asked about coming early to do some fishing. Shooter agreed and told him he would open the gate.

Once the call was completed, Jessie finished eating and paid for his meal. He drove back to his place to get his rod and reel and to make sure everything was ready for tonight. Remote listening device, 9mm with silencer, and sniper rifle with scope. Now he was ready, and his next stop was the lake.

When Jessie got to the lake, he parked behind the garage, which put the house on the other side. He backed the car in so he would be ready for a fast take off. He got out of the car, grabbed his fishing rod, and knocked on the door which was quickly opened by Shooter who said, "How about a cold beer before you test the water."

"Shooter," Jessie said, "now maybe that's what was wrong the last time, no beer. Thought this time I'd try the other side of the lake."

"That might help," Shooter said, "and how about a sandwich to go with the drink."

"OK Shooter, and let's shoot the breeze for awhile," Jessie said.

While Shooter was making the sandwiches, Jessie sat down at the table and took a swallow of his beer and said, "What do you think about the Uterio brothers dying?"

Shooter answered with, "Oh, I don't know Jessie. Could have happened like they say it did, but I'm not so sure. Of course, if they lose any more guys, they won't need this place to meet, so guess I'll retire once they close this place down. I understand Romeo is taking over their people, so there's no loss of business."

"Looks like pretty good leadership when someone kicks the bucket and yet everything else goes on undisturbed—or perhaps it's just good planning in the event of an emergency. We both have our own idea of what happened, and we'd best keep it to ourselves. Did you hear that? Think the fish just called to me so I'll go try my luck. If I don't have any, I'll come back for another beer, if you don't mind."

Shooter grabbed a couple beers and said, "I'll come out with you and even carry your drink. Maybe I'll bring you some luck!"

Jessie made a couple casts with the rod and then asked, "How did you get tied up with this crew Shooter?"

"Remember the Gulardi family we talked about? I worked for them running a gambling hall until they got killed. Later I went to work doing the same thing for the Uterio brothers, and when they needed someone to take care of this place, I took it."

"Let me guess," Jessie said, "Dice was your game, hence the nickname, Shooter?"

"Yes," Shooter said, "and damn good. Never used crooked dice so no one really missed me when I came here."

A couple hours went by, and Jessie finally put up his rod and said, "Damn, only a couple strikes and nothing big so it's time to call it quits."

"You still got a couple hours so why not watch some TV for awhile."

Jessie responded with, "I could, as long as I'm out here before they come."

"No worry there," Shooter said, "Leo always calls just before they start on their way out here."

"Good idea, Shooter," Jessie said, "I don't want to get in the way 'cause the grapevine says they got a visitor that's going to be here".

"He's already here," Shooter said, "came in yesterday late and stayed here with me. He went out to look around right before you got here. One mean-looking bastard, if you ask me. Not that he's so big, but he's got stone-cold eyes and reminds me of a wise-guy by the way he talks and moves."

"I understand he came here for the meeting to see how all these crews work together," Jessie said. "Look how simple it would be if all the big cities were controlled by only one Gang Lord. This could sweep through the entire country and the power one man would have is unbelievable. Hell, he could control hundreds."

The time they spent watching TV and drinking beer passed quickly. Both men were startled when Shooter's cell phone rang.

"Shooter here, what's up? Oh, excuse me sir, thirty minutes? We'll be ready."

"I heard that Shooter so I'll take one to go and be ready when Chico gets here."

Jessie went out back to his car and removed the shotgun he had, along with the small remote that he put in his pocket. Then he placed the small listening recorder and one ear receiver under his shirt. He went to the edge of the lake and sat down to wait for Chico.

A few minutes later a car pulled in and parked in front of the garage. A man Jessie had never seen stepped out. This was the visitor from out of state. Next, Leo's car pulled in, and both men went inside. With no one in sight, Jessie placed the listening device into his ear and knew if he saw anyone coming, he could remove it. Jessie moved to the left of the garage and wondered if something was wrong with his bug because nothing was coming through his ear piece.

Suddenly the door opened, and he heard Leo say, "The others will be here soon so let's go down and get comfortable. Dad was right about you knowing your job—that fire was perfect. The other two you'll meet tonight. How they go, we don't care. Just make it soon, and by the way, tomorrow Dad has a present for you—pay for all four."

Just then Jessie saw some cars pulling in so he took out his earpiece but left the small recorder on. He put the earpiece into his picket and watched as the two cars stopped in front of the house. Chico drove by to the other side where Jessie had parked the last time. Once parked, two more men went into the house, and Chico waved in Jessie's direction. Jessie realized that Chico wasn't coming over so he returned the listening device to his ear. Although he couldn't tell who was speaking when he heard, "Nice to see you boys. This is Troy and he was sent here to look us over. Tonight we need to discuss filling or not filling the brothers' place. We want to know how you boys feel about it. Romeo will be here pretty soon and can give you all the details in full on how things look. We can then vote so we're all on the same page. Of course, with them gone, the split is bigger."

"How's this new Lead Man idea working out? Hell, if I didn't have the pool hall, I wouldn't have much to do."

"I can't speak for Mick here, but I like it. He takes good care of the businesses and gives me plenty of free time."

"Me too, at first it bothered me, but now, as you say, I can go and know things are running good".

"See what I was talking about Troy? Like Dad said, by us working together like we are, this outfit will run itself. Let me call Romeo. If you boys like the way we're going, we can vote now, and he can stay home."

The call was placed to Romero and he said, "You can forget about coming, everything is cool here."

Jessie had heard enough. As he headed toward his car, he removed the remote and flipped the switch.

The sound was deafening as the house disintegrated. As Jessie turned, he threw the remote as far out into the lake as was humanly possible. As he looked around, he saw Chico and knew he was dead. Where a house once stood, there was now only rubble. He saw Shooter stretched out behind where the house had once been.

Jessie jumped into his car, took off through the gate, and was soon turning off on a side road. Only one more place to go and that was to Leo's. Now he knew who was the "brains" of the outfit. It was Leo's Dad.

He parked the car in the same place he had before. He got out, opened the trunk, and removed the 9mm pistol with its silencer. Once this was accomplished, his job would be done here.

As he approached the house, he noticed the lights were on the same as before. As he looked through the window, he saw Leo's dad and Romero sitting on the couch. It was over for Leo's dad, almost before the glass broke. When he fired his second shot, Romero fell as if struck by an axe. Jessie stuck his hand through the broken window, unlocked it and went inside.

He found a ledger and some other books in the desk. He removed a pillowcase from the pillow now on the floor and put the ledger and books inside. He was ready to leave but noticed two large briefcases—and decided they might contain important information so he took them too. Before he left, he made sure there was nothing identifying him that was left behind.

Once he got back to his car and checked to make sure that no one was around, he opened the trunk and put everything that he had taken from Leo's house under a blanket there. Tomorrow he would go through everything and send most or all of it to his contact.

When Jessie got back to his place, he called his contact. When the voice answered, he said, "I want you to know I'm sending you a package overnight. Better have your people ready to move as my job is over so I'll give you a call later on."

"OK, only one question. Who was Number One?"

"Well," Jessie said, "when I had decided it was Leo, I was ready to move. Turned out I was only partly right; it was his dad. You'll get a tape in the mail that tells how the Uterio Brothers met their end and how his dad planned to take out the other two bosses."

"Sounds like it's all we need, how about you?" Jessie's contact asked. "Any complications or are you in the clear?"

"No way I can be tied to what happened," Jessie said. "All steps were thought out well in advance, and anyway, whoever did the job must have been smart. All joking aside, the old man named Shooter was only a gambler who took care of the house after he lost his job. Look after him if you can. He was ready to retire and not in the business, just the caretaker".

"We'll do what we can," his contact said, "although I don't know what can be done. Give me a call in a day or two, in case we have any questions."

"I'll call, but just remember, I'm going to disappear for a while so until then, take care of yourself."

Jessie hung up the phone, got a cold beer and turned on the TV.

All of a sudden, the news came on and the announcer said, "The explosion killed five people and the first reports indicate a gas leak set it off. From all indications, there were no survivors. Four were inside the house and the fifth was found outside."

This was welcome news to Jessie. Evidently Shooter must have been stunned by the blast, and once he came to, saw the rubble of the place and left before anyone got there.

Jessie's mind went back to the news. "Due to the conditions of some of the bodies found, an autopsy will be performed, and the families notified before releasing the names of the victims."

Jessie turned off the TV and knew they would find Leo's dad and Romero once they had identified Leo's body. Then they might tie in the explosion to the killings unless they determined that the gas had exploded by accident. Jessie couldn't believe how he was feeling as his mind went through all that had transpired. The adrenaline was pumping so hard through his body that he felt truly alive! Then his thoughts went to Francine.

How long could his Francine, his one true love, keep him from needing more excitement?

When he was with her, nothing else mattered, but what would she say if she knew what he did for the government?

Damn it, how could they start a life together when she knew nothing about him? Tomorrow they would have a long talk. He would tell her the truth about his life, and Francine would have the final word. Could she accept him knowing his past? With all his heart he wanted her, but knew he would give her up if he had to.

Unable to come down off his "high," he walked out to the car and brought in the full pillowcase along with the two briefcases. He shook the contents of the pillowcase out on the bed and looked over what he had: two notebooks, one diary, and a large stack of papers. He wasn't interested in any of the contents so he placed the items in the largest of the envelopes he had ready to mail and sealed it.

Jessie set the envelope aside, picked up the smallest briefcase, and jimmied the lock. As he lifted the top on the briefcase, he couldn't believe his eyes as he stared at the stacks of one hundred dollar bills! This was the payoff for the work that had been done on the two brothers.

Jessie counted the stacks. There were seven long and two deep, a total of fourteen. Hard to believe there was that much money in that small case. A dollar is two and a half inches by six inches, and each stack was three inches tall. Not caring how much was there, he closed the case and opened the larger one.

Here too, was a surprise! Lying on top was a plane ticket to Stockholm, Sweden. Jessie opened the ticket and found it was a round trip ticket for Leo. Underneath that were two stacks of negotiable bonds and beside them were four stacks of bills. Leo's trip must have been planned to set up a bank account.

Jessie closed the case but retained the ticket, which he destroyed. No one would know about the contents of the cases until he decided what to do. As he put both cases into the closet, his mind went once again to Francine. Not telling her the truth was no longer a choice, but he knew that leaving out some of the details might soften some of the shock she would feel. After all, had it not gone another way, her uncles would have been at the meeting too.

Jessie felt no remorse for what he had done. In his eyes, they were all killers in their own way. His method was fast and final—and not a slow death that drugs imposed on people, the young especially. He also thought about the many deaths they had ordered and were responsible for. No, he felt justified in what he had done, and they deserved the just reward he had handed to them.

With the adrenaline still pumping, Jessie drank a few more beers before trying to sleep. When he finally closed his eyes, the next thing he saw was the sunlight coming through his window and realized that he had slept a peaceful sleep.

After a quick shower, he drove to Mom and Pop's Restaurant for breakfast. He called Francine and asked if she would like to take a drive.

She responded with "Yes, my love, are we driving to Las Vegas I hope?"

"We'll go honey, but not today," Jessie said. "I just want to hold you and talk about the future so I'll be there in about thirty minutes. See you then."

With breakfast over and the bill paid, Jessie drove to Francine's house, and there, sitting on the porch swing, was the love of his life. Today would answer if she was to be his or not.

Before the car had stopped, she was at the curb waiting. As soon as he stopped, she opened the passenger door, slid into the seat and didn't stop until their lips met. As they parted, she said, "Where are we headed my man?"

"How about the beach at Atlantic City? We can talk on the way as there are some things I want you to know."

"This sound like it's really serious. I don't care what it is, as long as you love me like I love you."

"My dearest Francine," Jessie said, "In my life there have been only two people I would have gladly died for, my folks. They are both gone, and now you are the same to me as my parents were. You are the love of my life. You alone hold my heart but, I love you too much to marry you until you know what I do for the government. When you hear what I have to say, and if you still want to get married, then and only then can we go to Las Vegas. But you must promise me that whatever I tell you, will be held in the strictest confidence no matter what your decision might be regarding us.

"Jessie," Francine said, "I promise that whatever you tell me, I will forget it and will never repeat it. As serious as you are, don't you think I deserve a kiss before you begin your story?"

"Can we hold off for a couple minutes?" Jessie asked. "There's a roadside picnic area a couple miles down the road, and we can finish our talk, after our kiss."

The car was barely stopped when their lips met, and it was Jessie who finally pulled back.

"Damn woman, I'm trying to wait until we say "I do" but you've got to help me. All I can think about is having you as my wife when I can hold you and kiss you and explore your body and wanting to know that you feel the same."

"I do want you so much. I've never been with a man before, nor have I wanted to be until you came into my life. Now it seems so natural to be in your arms that I can't think of anything else either."

"Honey, I'm so sorry," Jessie said, "but God willing, we'll be one in spirit and body but first I must finish my story."

Francine gently touched his hand and then backed away toward her side of the car to listen to his story.

Jessie began.

"When I was discharged from the service, I was offered a job through the government that needed the special training I had received while in the military. I could have refused, but once it was offered and I had time to think about it, I decided to take on the job.

"In a lot of big cities, there are many gangs. Just suppose one person was able to get them together and have them work as a team. His power would be unstoppable, and his word would be law. If the right palms in the right places were greased, no one could touch him.

"My job is to find him and remove him from office, but in the meantime, I have to become one of them until I can find him. Therein lies the danger of the job. It is my responsibility to pass information to others regarding anyone I meet who might fit the criteria or is involved with the man I'm trying to remove from office. Until I call in, I'm unemployed because only a few know what I do. Everything else I've ever told you is the truth."

Francine had listened to his story and asked, "By not calling in, what would you do?"

"Remember I told you that money is no problem? My folks left me well off and the only reason I took the job was for the danger element. My life was very humdrum with no excitement; then the army made me come alive by introducing me to something I enjoyed."

"Since you would give that up for me," Francine said, "I need a promise from you. If you ever feel you want to return to that kind of work, you will give them a call."

Jessie couldn't believe his ears! She had actually understood that someday he might need to return to the business and was willing to open her heart for that potential need. How could he be so lucky to have found such a beautiful and understanding woman?

"Thank you, my love, I don't think that will ever happen, but if it does, I promise, you'll be the first to know. With that settled, my question to you is: 'Do you want to drive or fly to Las Vegas?'"

"I've never been west, only east so I'd like us to drive so we can enjoy the country between here and there."

"Then drive we will," Jessie said, "It's about three day's driving so when do you want to leave?"

"How about in the morning," Francine said, "this would get us there and ready when Mom and Dad fly out."

"OK, let me turn around so we can get home and get ready for our trip. I'll pick you up around five a.m., is that OK?"

"If I didn't want to tell my folks, we could leave right now," Francine said.

"I'm glad you want to tell your folks, Francine," Jessie said, "because I have to pack and check out of my place."

Once back at Francine's, both went in to see her parents. Francine was all aglow and said, "Mom, we're leaving in the morning so we can drive. I'll call you when we get there so you can tell us when you'll be arriving."

Francine's folks were excited and wished them well and all the normal conversation that goes with well-wishing.

"Sweetheart, I have a lot to do before we leave, so I'll take off," Jessie finally said. "See you in the morning around five. I love you.

I'll say goodbye for a short while Mom and Dad. Please don't worry, I'll take good care of her."

After kissing Francine goodbye, Jessie drove to the UPS office and sent everything overnight. He then went looking for a place to service the car for the upcoming trip and spotted a Jiffy Lube. When he entered the office, he got quite a start because there, waiting for his own car, was Shooter.

"Thank God you got away too. I'm sorry but when I saw Chico dead, I thought you were too so I took off. I figured when the cops got there, some of their questions would be hard to answer."

"Me too", Shooter said, "When I came to, I jumped in my car and got out of there. Then I realized I was supposed to be there so I went back. The fire department showed up fifteen minutes later, along with a cop car and two detectives. They saw Chico when they drove up, and once they put out the fire, they found the rest. Looks like the gas caused the explosion, and I was glad that you got away. There were a lot of questions, and they're trying to identify all the remains they found. So far they think only four were in the house, but with the damage, they're still looking. Looks like I've retired, although I'll still have to find some way to make ends meet. How come you're still in town? I thought you'd be long gone by now".

"Shooter," Jessie said, "I'm taking off, but I run across jobs all the time that I know you could do, honest jobs. How about giving me your address, and if I run across any, I'll drop you a line?"

"Thank you Jessie," Shooter said, "I would gladly accept your help. The rest of those who didn't make it were good riddance, but I'm glad you weren't one of them. Why, with all you got going for you, why don't you look for another kind of work? Also, if you drop me a line, let me know how to get in touch because someday I'll remember who you remind me of—and while it was someone I liked, for the life of me, I can't place who it was."

"Shooter, by tomorrow I'll be gone, but I'll let you know how to get in touch, once I get there," Jessie said.

Just then they told Shooter that his car was ready, and after paying his bill, he handed Jessie a paper with his address and phone number. "I've got to get back out there," Shooter said, "So you take care of yourself, and maybe someday I'll see you again."

"Only God knows that answer Shooter, and I hope we'll meet again also. In any case, I'll call you in a few days to see how this all turns out. Until then, you be careful and stay out of trouble."

Jessie watched Shooter's car until it was almost out of sight, thinking all the while how grateful he was that Shooter had made it safely out of the blast from the house. His thoughts were broken when the garage mechanic told him his car was ready. Jessie realized it was time for him to hit the road too.

Once he was back home, he turned on the television and began gathering his small amount of belongings together. The news was on, and they were talking about finding two men shot. Evidently they went to notify them about the death of the man that lived there, namely Leo, and that's when they found the bodies of Leo's dad and Romero. These shooting deaths were also under investigation. Only time would tell if Jessie had left any clues or forensics leads of himself behind.

Jessie pulled out his suitcases and put everything from the closet and drawers on the bed. Packing came easy as he had room left over in one of the cases for other things. He took the bonds and money from both the brief cases and neatly hid it in with his clothes except for a couple stacks that he would mail anonymously to Shooter.

Next, he placed five month's rent into an envelope and laid the envelope on the kitchen table. His lease was now paid in full. Pat and Lee deserved the money. He found his tablet and wrote a note to Pat and told her the money would be on the table. He thanked both Pat and Lee for being such good landlords and friends and then told them goodbye. In the morning, the note would be in the mailbox.

Jessie laid out the clothes he would wear tomorrow and set his alarm for four thirty a.m., turned off the TV, took a quick shave, and enjoyed a long relaxing shower before turning in for the night. He was up before the alarm went off and quickly dressed. He carried the two bags and envelope down the steps and placed the envelope, along with the apartment keys into the mail box. After putting the suitcases into the trunk, he returned to the apartment for a last check. He picked up the two empty briefcases that he'd cleaned well and let the door lock behind him as he left. He placed the two briefcases in the seat beside him. When he passed a dumpster, he threw both wiped cases away. Sometime tonight, he would mail the package to Shooter, but now he had to pick up his traveling companion, the love of his life.

Chapter 32

When Jessie arrived at Francine's house, he noticed that the lights were on inside so he pulled into the driveway, knocked on the door and went in, not waiting for someone to open the door for him. There sat Mom, Pop and Francine, all drinking coffee.

"How about some breakfast before you kids leave?" Mom said.

"No Mom," Jessie said, "you both go back to bed, and we'll stop to eat later. Honey, I'll put your bags in the car while you say your good-byes to your folks. Pop, we'll see you Friday when we pick you up at the airport. You and Mom have a nice flight."

Jessie carried the bags to the car and returned for Francine who was just coming out the door, followed by her parents.

"You kids have a safe trip. Jessie, don't let her be the boss," Pop said and laughed.

Francine responded with, "Dad, I told you that for now, I'm letting him think he's the boss so don't tell him that."

"It's alright sir," Jessie said, "I'm so used to being told what to do. I let them think they're the boss. You ready honey 'cause its time to hit the road."

"Yes, I'm ready to begin the rest of my life with you," and they drove away amongst the farewells, 'I love you' and 'we'll see you Friday' to her parents.

Jessie explained the trip plan to Francine, telling her they would be taking three highways to Las Vegas. The #76 which turned into the #70 and then on to the #15 which they would hit in Utah. "If we put in a long day today, we could spend the night in Kansas. What do you think about that?"

"Drive on my love," Francine said, "like I told my Dad, you're the boss."

They drove for the next several hours and around eight in the morning, they stopped at a rest area for gas and for some breakfast. They talked quietly as they ate, with each gazing into the other's eyes, knowing that their love would soon come to fruition as they traveled toward their marriage and life together as one. Knowing that time was flying by, they finally returned to the car and began the next portion of their trip, stopping only one more time for a healthy lunch and more gas.

Much later that night, they stopped in Junction City, Kansas and Jessie said, "Well, my love, that was one hell of a drive but one more day like today, then a short day and we'll be in Vegas. There's a Howard Johnson's. We can get a couple rooms there."

Francine agreed, leaned over and put her head on his shoulder until they arrived at the motel.

They walked in with their luggage up to the check-in counter. Jessie asked for two rooms on the same floor. They were informed that there was a pair of adjoining rooms, if that would be suitable. Both Jessie and Francine agreed, took their keys, and went to the floor where their rooms were located. Jessie opened Francine's door for her. They both walked into her room, with Jessie checking to make sure the room was acceptable for her, which it was.

"Honey, why don't you freshen up," Jessie said, "and I'll do the same. We can order room service for some dinner and perhaps some wine."

Francine said she wasn't terribly hungry but that would be nice. They shared a quick kiss, and then Jessie left to check out his own room.

Once in his room, Jessie decided to call his contact and ask for a favor. When his call was answered, Jessie asked him about mailing a package to Shooter, as he didn't want anyone to know where he was headed. Jessie said, "I hope my package to you got them started because if they wait too long, someone else might come in and take over."

"Not to worry," his contact said, "we had people in place by Monday waiting for our call to snafu the business or what was left of it. By the way, Jessie, awhile back you asked me about Gulardi, still interested?"

"Sure am, although I found out some things, like the guy the package is for, he used to work for them."

"Raymond Gulardi was the patriarch of the clan," his contact said. "He was well educated and a top-notch businessman. It seems that all but a young grandson were killed by the people who took over all his assets—except the bank account and a safety deposit box, also in the bank. Anyway, this grandson could own the factory and any other properties, as they feel the Uterio brothers used fraud to obtain them. Hell, the money alone is staggering so the kid is rich beyond belief. Another thing, after twenty years, the bank turns it over to the government, which is about three more years. How did you get so interested?"

Jessie responded with, "I heard a boy talking one day and got inquisitive. The only thing now, is how could he prove who he is?"

"That's the easy part," his contact replied. "The hospital where he was born has his fingerprints and footprints, so if this boy thinks he might be the Gulardi grandson, tell him to get a good lawyer and go for it."

"Thanks for all the info," Jessie said, "I'll be in touch before too long so you be good. So long for now."

Jessie put down the phone and headed for the shower. Talk about things to think about. He had enough for a couple people, but for the next few weeks, he'd put it out of his mind.

When Jessie finished his shower, he dressed and knocked on the adjoining door to Francine's room and she said, "Come in."

As Jessie opened the door, what he saw literally took his breath away. Francine was standing there in a beautiful white satin and lace nightgown partially covered by a white satin robe. Her long dark hair framed her beautiful face and fell over her shoulders to a length that all but covered her breasts. He couldn't decide if she looked like an angel or a goddess standing there but was immediately aroused at the sight of her. As he glanced around, he saw that the bed covers were pulled back to expose the white sheets on which they were about to lay. He walked into the room, and as he did, she slowly walked toward him. They embraced and began kissing. Jessie knew that they would not have to wait another day or night to enjoy their honeymoon night.

Jessie's head was spinning as he touched her and caressed her. As he did so, she began unbuttoning his shirt, and as his shirt came off, Jessie removed her satin robe. She began helping him unzip and remove his trousers. All the while, their passion rose until Jessie picked her up in his arms and laid her beautiful body on what was to be their wedding bed. Their lovemaking was slow and gentle as they explored and caressed each other's bodies until their passion grew to a point that Jessie didn't think he could hold out much longer. He felt her pulling him to her, and as he gently entered her virgin body, she let out a cry that was a combination of pain and pleasure. They were now one with each other, and as their passion rose, they were both brought to the pinnacle together when Francine let out a moan. Jessie knew she had reached her peak, and he could no longer hold back his passion and exploded within her.

As the passion waned, Jessie looked down upon her and kissed her lips, her eyes, and her neck. He told her how beautiful she looked with the flush of love on her face and told her how much he loved her. Her eyelids were half closed, and she gazed at him through the fringes of her beautiful, long dark eyelashes and told him how wonderful was his lovemaking and how much she loved him. As Jessie moved to the side, he took her in his arms and holding each other, they both soon fell asleep.

In the morning, they were awakened with the phone ringing for their requested wake-up call. Jessie answered and responded with, "Yes, I'm awake." Jessie turned to his bride-to-be and was still amazed at her beauty. As they kissed, their passion was stirred again, and once more, they made passionate love but this time it was even more intense. Francine was more aggressive, and they were soon spent once again.

They really wanted to spend the day in bed but knew that they would have to get back on the road in order to reach Las Vegas on schedule. Jessie reluctantly left the bed to return to his own room to shower and dress. Francine did the same in her own room. When Francine finally got out of the shower and dressed, she looked upon the bed and around the room with fondness and knew that the memory of that room and that bed would remain in her memory forever. In this place she had spent her wedding night entwined in the arms of the man that she loved and whom she would soon call her husband. She smiled as the memories of last night and this morning engulfed her. She was sorry they had to leave so soon, but she knew there would be a lifetime of lovemaking ahead for them both.

Francine knocked on the door that separated her and Jessie. He opened the door quickly. She was at once in his arms again, and their kisses were passionate. Jessie had to remind her that they still had a long drive through Colorado so they agreed to leave their love nest and go to the restaurant for breakfast before continuing on their journey. As they ate breakfast, Jessie explained to Francine that today they would have another long day of driving, but because the following day would be a short drive, they could stay longer in the motel tomorrow morning.

Francine found that Jessie had been right about the long drive. They had stopped only a couple times to gas up the car, make a potty stop, and grab a few snacks to munch on as they traveled. When they finally reached their day's destination, both were quite exhausted from the long trip.

Jessie checked into the hotel, but this time requested only one room. While he secured the room and carried their luggage in, Francine waited for him in the restaurant. They were tired from all the traveling but enjoyed a nice dinner and each other's company while they ate. When they finished their meal, Jessie paid the bill, and they walked toward their room together. Francine was pleased because it was a lovely room, tastefully decorated, with the point of interest being a beautifully made, king-sized bed. Jessie asked Francine if she would like to shower first or if she wanted him to shower first. He didn't miss the little smile on her face when she suggested that they shower together.

That night, along with the night before, would never be forgotten by either one. Sharing the shower only started the unbelievable passion that would continue through the night. While Jessie began soaping, rinsing, and kissing Francine's body, she was doing the same with him. They were caught up in the smell and taste of one another and before they were completely dry, found themselves once again on the bed with the exploring and caressing continuing until they could not restrain themselves any longer. Francine was almost begging Jessie to enter her. He did so trying to be gentle, but their passion was so great that he allowed himself to follow her lead and drove himself deep within her. As he did so, their moans blended together in oneness as they both reached the peak of their passion. It wasn't until Jessie collapsed beside her that he realized they had been making love for hours. He couldn't believe the time had flown by so quickly, but he just couldn't get enough of her and realized that she felt the same about him.

Despite their long hours of lovemaking, they were both wide awake at six a.m. With her head on Jessie's arm, Francine said, "Don't you think we should rehearse a little more before we get married? You know, being new at this, I'd like to get it right."

"Honey, I don't know how you could get any better. You are all woman, and I love you so." As Jessie had been talking to Francine, he had also been touching her as he spoke, and she had been touching him. Jessie was erect once again so as Francine had requested, they rehearsed again with all the passion as before.

Chapter 33

Later, they were driving on Highway #70 where they picked up #15 with a straight shot to Las Vegas and arrived early that afternoon. Jessie exited on Tropicana and headed for the Luxor that he had found on the Internet. Jessie parked close to the registration door. He and Francine went in and were able to get rooms for both themselves and Francine's parents. They had decided that they would wait until tomorrow to get the marriage license and have it with them when they picked up her parents at the airport. From there, they would head straight to a wedding chapel for the ceremony. While checking in, Jessie checked with the desk clerk about overnight UPS service and was assured that the package would go out that day, if he could get it to them before 3pm.

Once in the room, Jessie removed the envelope addressed to Shooter and asked Francine if she would order their meal via room service while he went back downstairs to send the package. When Jessie arrived at the front desk, he asked for a larger envelope and addressed it to his contact in Virginia and put the envelope addressed to Shooter inside. Once it arrived in Virginia, his contact would remove the envelope and mail it on to Shooter; thereby leaving no trace of the exact point of origin. With the mailing in order, he gave the desk clerk $20 as a combination mailing fee and tip for the service and said he would pick up his receipt later.

When Jessie returned to the room, he could hear the shower running and knew Francine would be there. He couldn't wait to jump in the shower with her. Even he was surprised at how quickly he could rid himself of his clothes when he had thoughts of his bride-to-be on his mind. Once in the shower, he took her in his arms and was ready for her again, but she teased him and said, "Too late my love, the food is on the way up, but at least I've got a new place to hang my washcloth"! With that she laughed and jumped out of the shower. Talk about bursting a bubble!

The washcloth quickly hit the shower floor, and Jessie said, "OK honey, you win this one but lookout next time 'cause you won't be able to get away that easy. But since you've made your great escape, take the money out of my wallet so you can pay for the food when it arrives. I'll be out in a few minutes.

When Jessie finished his shower, he joined Francine at the small table in their room and they had a light mid-day lunch.

"Jessie, you mentioned that you'd like to have a nice meal downstairs this evening. Is that still what you want to do?"

"Francine, I love you dearly and want you to know about my past, and the journey we are about to embark upon. To begin, the name that you know me by, Jessie Ruben is my adopted name. I would like for us to be married with that name so you will become Mrs. Jessie Ruben. However, the people in Virginia that I work for may know my real identity. Once we're married, I'd like to go back and find out for sure. Will it bother you to find out that my name is something other than Jessie Ruben?"

As Francine looked lovingly at her beloved one, all she could say was, "Jessie, I'm not marrying you because of your name. I'm marrying you because you are the man I have fallen deeply in love with and want to spend the rest of my life with. If you find out that you carry a different name than Ruben, I'll carry it with you if that be your desire."

"I was hoping that would be your answer, Francine. And with that Jessie hugged her tightly and said, "Why don't you call Mom and see what time we're supposed to pick them up. Let them know that we'll be getting married within a couple hours after they arrive."

Francine was so excited and jumped at the chance to call her mom to give her the good news. Once she hung up the phone, she told Jessie that their plane would be arriving and 11:20 tomorrow morning and added, "Mom says don't forget the marriage license."

"Honey, first thing in the morning, we'll go to the court house for the license and then to a chapel to make arrangements for the flowers, music and of course, a time. I was thinking that rather than go straight from the airport to the chapel, we should give your folks a chance to get settled into their room so what do you think about having the ceremony about 6 pm?"

Francine nodded in agreement and then Jessie said, "If there is anything you want to do tonight, go ahead as it's your last night as a single woman."

"I don't have any single woman plans, but I thought I might walk around some of the clothing shops downstairs. Perhaps I can pick up a few things for some future evenings we'll be spending together."

Jessie told her that it would be good for her to get out for awhile. Once Francine left the room, he put all the cash into one briefcase and put the bonds under his clothes in his suitcase. He would wire some of the money tomorrow and decided to donate the bonds to some charities. The charities would benefit from the bonds, and he would eventually donate all the cash which would, in a sense, clean up the dirty money. No one would ever know where it came from. Since Jessie didn't need any money, he wouldn't keep any of it for himself.

The next day went smooth as silk. With marriage license in hand, they went to the bank where Jessie took care of the cash, and on to the wedding chapel to make arrangements for the ceremony. From there, they went straight to the airport to pick up Francine's parents. Like the perfect day it was, the plane was right on time. After hugs all around, they drove to the hotel so they could get the folks checked in, and all could clean up for the wedding.

As they all left their rooms and walked into the casino, watching Francine's parents was like looking at two kids with a new toy. Their eyes were wide with wonder as they entered this Casino world: all the lights flashing, all the people and the noise from the ringing and clanging of the machines, and the sound of the money dropping into trays all around. For this older couple who had worked so hard all their lives, it was like a playground just for them. They were entranced with the wonder of it all.

Jessie knew he had to get them out before they tried one game or none of them would make it to the chapel.

"I knew you would be impressed with these casinos, and you can spend all the time in here you want after the ceremony. Right now, however, we'll have to go 'cause we don't want to be late for our own wedding."

Francine's folks looked at Jessie. He could tell they felt a little sheepish for almost forgetting their own daughter's wedding because they were so impressed with all the hustle and bustle inside the casino.

They arrived at a lovely wedding chapel where Jessie had left no stone unturned to make this the most memorable occasion for his beautiful bride. He had ordered special music, flowers for all, and a gorgeous bouquet for his Francine. It was a lovely ceremony and seemed to go by quickly until Mr. and Mrs. Jessie Ruben were sharing their first kiss as husband and wife. Francine's dad was shaking Jessie's hand and said, "Jessie, I'm so very happy to welcome you into our family and so happy to finally have a son." There were hugs and kisses all around, and they decided to have their wedding dinner at a buffet. Francine's folks had never seen a buffet so huge with so many choices so they took their time discussing the wonderful food that was laid out for them to select.

Once they were finally all seated and began eating, Francine's dad asked what their future plans were, now that they were married.

Jessie told them about his adoption, and the fact that the people in Virginia had clues to his true identity. He and his new bride planned to drive back to Virginia to seek out the truth once and for all.

"While we drive back," Jessie said, "it will give you and Mom plenty of time to look around and perhaps you'll decide that you like it here." Jessie handed his new father-in-law a beeper and said, "We want you to have this so Francine can keep in touch as you don't have a cell phone yet. This way she can let you know where to call us."

Pop was really enjoying the buffet food and said, "Gambling must bring in a lot of money to let people eat so cheap."

"That's for sure Pop," Jessie said. "Only the Government takes in more money than gaming does. They could give the food away and still make money. Most people spend a good amount of money on their way out of town, I guess in the hope that they'll recap all the monies they've spent so far; but believe me, they don't build all these huge casinos on the winners. By the way, what are your plans once Francine and I leave for Virginia?"

"We'll probably relax a few days and take in some sights and shows, then buy a car and start checking around. We'll probably drive over to California and see what's available and where. We've never been to California so we'll just take our time and enjoy ourselves before making any final decisions on where we want to plant roots. In any case, if we lose contact for some reason, have Francine call Aunt Helen. She'll know where we're at. They'll be staying put until both their place and ours is sold. Once we get settled, they'll join us wherever that might be."

With the meal concluded, Jessie said, "Well folks, don't mean to rush, but Francine and I would like to get on the road. We're planning to drive as far as St. George tonight so we'd better get going."

Francine kissed her parents goodbye and said, "Well Mom and Dad, we're off to begin our life together so don't worry, I'll call in a couple days".

"I'll always worry but at least now that you're married and have Jessie to watch over you, it will be much easier. You kids take your time and drive careful," Mom said.

"Don't worry Mom, I'll take good care of her," Jessie said. "You take good care of each other until we get back. We'll call you soon."

With that, Jessie and Francine went to their hotel room to get their luggage and begin their trip.

Once on the road, Francine asked, "How long will it take us to get to St. George, Jessie? After all honey, it's our honeymoon, and I just love to cuddle." As she was talking, she was reaching over touching her new husband and could feel his firm manhood pressing against his trousers. She started to unzip his pants.

"Whoa baby, slow down a little. I'm anxious to hold you too so rather than drive to St. George, we'll stop in Mesquite. That's only a few more miles so hold off for just a little longer."

Francine giggled and teased him a bit more, but let the poor man concentrate on his driving.

That night and for the next three nights, Francine was more than happy with their journey and with their lovemaking at every opportunity. They were madly in love with each other and made such a wonderful couple with their passions so evenly matched. On the fourth day, they arrived at their destination in Virginia. They stopped at Williamsburg, Virginia and decided to spend the night there, as the afternoon was almost gone. Jessie said, "Honey, I'll get up early and drive to the Camp Perry as it's only a short distance."

The next morning, Jessie let his new bride sleep as he shaved and showered for his drive to the base. He kissed her gently on the cheek and looked upon her sleeping form and was still in awe that this beauty was his wife. He loved her so very much.

Chapter 34

Jessie drove to the base and was stopped while the guard called ahead for permission. Once it was granted, Jessie continued to the same office as before, and the same man was waiting for him.

"Kind of looked for you yesterday, Jessie. What happened?"

"We decided not to hurry," Jessie said, "so we took in some scenery along the way. How did things turn out after I left?"

"Remember that warehouse? We made the gun bust we were looking for."

Jessie was surprised and said, "Gun bust? Where did the guns come from? Why didn't someone tell me about it?"

"Jessie," the man said, "that was how they laundered the drug money. They sold the guns, increased their profits, and the money was deposited in a bank overseas so there wasn't anyone who had to handle it. And don't forget, we're indirectly tied into the ATF, among other things. Now Jessie, why are you so interested in the Gulardi Family?"

"When my father passed away, there was information that he had left for me which included a letter from him and my Mom telling me that I had been adopted. Naturally, it was a shock to me because I never knew or even had an inkling that they weren't my real parents. The letter said that my real name is Raymond Gulardi, and my real parents were murdered. If it's all true, I have questions that need to be answered so I want to find out for sure."

"That could be dangerous for you Jessie," the man said, "after all, some of their old enemies might still be around."

"That could be true, although I think their killers are dead. I do have one 'Ace in the hole' though. Remember that package you sent for me? Well, Shooter worked for my real father and knows who to look out for."

"Ken Walls, or Shooter, as you call him," the man said, "was high up with the Gulardi clan. He may know where some of the skeletons are buried. We've seriously considered recruiting him to work with us so you came to us at just the right time. One more thing Jessie, if the hospital proof is in route, they can still take DNA samples, even after twenty years.

"There is also a rumor that some guy by the name of Scott is trying to take over what's left of the crew that got away. Seems there wasn't any evidence against him. However, it now appears that he ran an enforcement gang, is pretty smart, and an ex-ranger, I heard".

"I saw him a couple times at the restaurant. He could throw a kink in my plans. I'll get with Shooter before I go in."

"What about your new wife, Jessie?" the man said. "She could be in danger along with you."

Jessie was thoughtful for a minute and said, "Maybe not back there in Philadelphia. Only her parents and her Aunt and Uncle know that we're married so until this is settled, we'll have to keep it quiet. May I use your phone to call Shooter?"

"Go right ahead," the man said.

Jessie dialed Shooter's number but only the answering machine came on so Jessie said, "Shooter, it's me Jessie. I'll call you later tonight around seven. I hope that we can get together real soon as I've got some real important issues to discuss with you".

Jessie turned to the man, thanked him for the use of the phone and said, "I'll try calling Shooter a little later but right now, I have to get back to my wife before she thinks I got lost. Thanks again. I'll be talking to you soon, and please keep me posted if anything else turns up."

When Jessie returned to the hotel, Francine was watching TV. Jessie walked over to her and took both her hand in his and said, "Honey, we're going to have to take you to your Aunt and Uncle's place in Philly. I've just found out that this could be dangerous for you if I am, in fact, a Gulardi. The Gulardi family was murdered years ago, and there may be some old enemies still out there. That's why I've called an old friend who used to work for my family. After all the killing, he looked after the lake property for the new people that took over."

"By the new people, you mean my dead uncles?"

"Yes honey," Jessie said, "but not only your uncles. There had to be many more involved. Ken should know who can and cannot be trusted. Perhaps he's got some inside information on how the takeover actually happened. Francine, there's something else I have to discuss with you, and I can't stress enough how important it is. Other than your Aunt, Uncle and your folks, no one, and I stress no one, is to know that we're married until I know it's safe for you."

Francine's eyes began to water and she asked, "Does this mean that our honeymoon is over already."

"No my darling," Jessie said, "our honeymoon is not over. I hope it will never be over, but right now, the most important thing to me is to keep you safe. We'll spend as much time together as we can but that time must be kept a secret—at least until we're sure that there's no one left to harm the last of the Gulardi family and his beautiful wife. For now honey, we've got to hit the road and drive close to your Aunt and Uncle. Tomorrow we'll go by their place so you can stay with them for the time being."

The time went by quickly as they drove and talked about their future together and how much they loved each other. Before they knew it, four hours had slipped by. They found a nice motel outside Camden and got a room for the night. Once settled in, Francine placed a call to her Mom via the beeper and a short time later her Mom called back. While Francine talked to her Mom, Jessie used his cell phone to place a call to Shooter.

The phone rang three times when Jessie heard his voice.

"Jessie here, Shooter," Jessie said, "I'm back and need to see you. How about Sal's around eight in the morning?"

"No problem," Shooter said, "do I need to carry anything or are you in trouble?"

"No trouble yet Shooter, but I need someone to watch my back. I'll explain the whole story to you when we meet. By the way, did you get your package?"

"Did I!" Shooter said. "There's no way I can repay you, but I'll sure try. See you at eight in the morning." With that done, Jessie looked toward Francine as she was just ending the call to her folks.

"The folks said to tell you hello," Francine said, "and Dad said he bought a car, got a cell phone, and they're headed to California. Boy, do they ever sound happy! Now to call Aunt Carol and Uncle Bob."

Laying in bed later that night after having made love yet again, they both knew that once Jessie dropped Francine off at her Aunt's place tomorrow, they would be apart for a few days or longer. Francine said, "How long will it take to find out if you really are a Gulardi?"

Jessie explained that if the hospital could locate his original birth certificate with the prints, it might be only a couple days.

"However," Jessie said, "if they can't prove it for us, then we might need a DNA sample from a body so I'd have to get a court order to exhume my father's body. In that case, it would take more time so we could take off someplace until it's done."

"What if you're not who you think you are?" Francine asked.

"If that's the case, then we'll head back toward Vegas as soon as we find out for sure." With that said, Jessie pulled his loving wife into his arms, kissed her and whispered "Good night my sweet" and both fell asleep.

The next morning, after dropping Francine off at her Aunt's place, Jessie drove to Sal's Restaurant to meet Shooter. Jessie was there only a couple minutes when Shooter walked through the door, spotted Jessie in the booth, and walked over. Jessie stood up to shake Shooter's hand, and it was obvious that both men were happy to see the other.

"Man, you look well rested and happy. Have things gone alright for you?" Shooter asked.

"Indeed they have Shooter," Jessie said, "and they might even get better. That's why I wanted to meet with you and perhaps hire you, if you're interested. Do you remember when you said I reminded you of someone?" Jessie lowered his voice and Shooter leaned toward him to hear better what Jessie was about to say.

"Shooter," Jessie said, "my foster parents used to work for the Gulardi Family and told me that I'm Raymond Gulardi Jr. It seems that the old man was my Grandfather and now, what I need to do is to prove whether or not it's true. The reason I've contacted you is the fact that you worked for the Gulardi's too, and you know who can be trusted and who might have been a part of the takeover in the first place."

The expression on Shooter's face was one of total disbelief and shock. You'd think he'd seen a ghost.

"Well Shooter," Jessie said, "What do you think?"

Shooter finally found his voice and said, "Lord, I have prayed all these years that the child would show up someday, but never did I dream it was you. As I sit here and look at you now, I can see the resemblance to your father and can't imagine why I didn't pinpoint it before; but once you prove it for sure, there are a lot of things you need to know."

"How do you think people will accept me if I am Raymond Gulardi?"

"Other than Scott and the crew he's forming," Shooter said, "I'd say that most will welcome you as a returning hero so I'll make some calls to a few guys that I know can be trusted all the way."

"Make your calls Shooter," Jessie said, "and we'll meet here the same time tomorrow. Don't worry about paying for the people you hire, that'll be taken care of. Just get as many as you think can be trusted, and as many as you think we'll need. One more thing Shooter, once this is over, I plan to leave you in charge of what once belonged to the Gulardi Family and keep things going right for me. I'll see you tomorrow."

Once Jessie was back in the car, he placed a call to Francine. "Hi honey, I hope you're enjoying the visit with your aunt and uncle. Since you are all familiar with this area, I need you to do me a favor, and it's very important."

"Whatever I can do to help, I'll do, you know that."

"Honey, I need you to find me a good, honest lawyer, someone we can trust with our lives, because that's what we'll be doing. See if I can get in to see him sometime today. I'll call you back in an hour for the info."

"Anything else you need Jessie?" Francine asked.

"No my love, that's all for now. Things are moving along quite well so I'll call sooner if anything else turns up, but at any rate, you'll hear from me in an hour. I love you."

Jessie hung up and drove straight to the hospital and asked to see the Director. After a short wait, he was shown into to the office of the Director, a Mr. Craft.

"Mr. Ruben," said Mr. Craft, "how can I be of assistance to you this morning?"

"Thank you for seeing me on such short notice Mr. Craft, but I am faced with a matter of some urgency. I need to know how long you keep records on births."

"Mr. Ruben, we've been very fortunate here as we've never had a fire or flood to destroy any of our records so we have files in our archives going back since the hospital was first built— and the first baby was born."

"So then it's possible," Jessie said, "for a person over twenty years later to prove his/her identity with a birth certificate held in your archives?"

"I would say yes," Mr. Craft said, "but the birth certificate would have the footprints of the baby and the identities of the parents. Tell me why you ask."

"A few months ago my foster parents died and left me information that indicated that I was born here around twenty years ago. You can imagine my surprise when I learned about this so I thought that with the assistance of a lawyer and the help of the hospital, I could validate that information."

"Well, you're starting off in the right direction," Mr. Craft said. "You will definitely need a lawyer as there are a lot of records that might be seen and could be considered an invasion of privacy if you didn't go about it in a legal manner. Once you get all the paperwork necessary, please come back, and we'll be happy to assist you in this matter, Mr. Ruben."

"Thank you so much for your time Mr. Craft," Jessie said. "I'll be in touch again, and I hope it will be soon. Have a good day Sir." Jessie returned to the car and called Francine.

"Hi Honey," Jessie said, "I'm a little early on this call but wondered if you had any news for me regarding a lawyer".

"Yes, I talked to my aunt and uncle. Uncle Bob gave me the name of an attorney that he swears by. His name is Ron Henderson, Attorney at Law." Francine gave Jessie the attorney's address and told him that an appointment had been arranged at twelve thirty. She said, "Will that time be OK with you Jessie?"

"Yes honey, that'll be great. I'll be there. How are the sales on the houses and businesses going?"

"Looks like only the houses will be left by the weekend so a Real Estate company will complete the sales even if my aunt and uncle aren't here," Francine said. "Once Mom and Dad call them, they are ready to go; in fact, Uncle Bob said if they don't call by next week, they're heading to Arizona and bought cell phones so they can keep in touch with my folks and us."

"It all sounds great Hon, like everything is really on track and going as we'd hoped and planned, but right now, I'd better get moving and check on the location of that attorney. I love you Mrs. Ruben and will call later tonight." After several other affectionate exchanges, Jessie hung up the phone and headed for the attorney's office.

Chapter 35

It wasn't difficult finding the attorney's office. Since it was still early, he decided to stop for a bite to eat before the appointment time. Jessie enjoyed nice restaurants and fine dining but he also liked some of the fast food chains. This time he decided on a chicken dinner with biscuits. Once his hunger had been satisfied, he felt much better and his mind was clear and his attitude upbeat. Things had been going along so well thus far, and he was eager to get his true identity revealed, despite the potential dangers that could come along with it.

Although it was still a little early for his appointment, he went to the attorney's office and saw a man who turned out to be Ron Henderson, talking with his secretary.

"Well hello, you must be Mr. Ruben," Ron Henderson said.

"Yes Sir, I hope I'm not too early."

"Not at all, I grabbed an early bite and just got back so come on back and have a seat."

Jessie was surprised to find that he liked this man. There was something about Ron Henderson that told Jessie that he could be trusted; and of course, the fact that Francine's uncle recommended him helped too.

Once seated in the office, Ron introduced himself and asked how he could be of service.

Jessie began his story.

"My foster parents left paperwork for me after they passed away. It indicated that I am actually the son of Raymond Gulardi and that I was born here twenty plus years ago. All of the Gulardi family, my family, were murdered. I have checked with the hospital, and they may have records of my birth. If not, we may have to have my father's body exhumed in order to get DNA samples to prove this Gulardi history. To accomplish this, I need a good attorney, and you come highly recommended as a man who can get things done. I need to find out the truth. Money is not an issue here."

Ron had listened intently to Jessie's story while taking a few notes and finally said, "I'd be happy to take your case, Mr. Ruben, but let's talk some more. First, you said that your whole family had been murdered. Were the killers ever caught, and does anyone know why they were killed?"

"Mr. Henderson, since you have agreed to take my case, could we please skip the formalities and would you please call me Jessie?"

With that Mr. Henderson laughed and said, "Agreed, and please call me Ron".

The two men were at ease with each other, and somehow knew their business relationship would continue for many years to come.

"Good, now to get on with the history of this whole situation. Apparently, the family was killed in what was a major take-over deal. The people that did the killing wanted the Gulardi land, businesses, and all possible assets. They did take over, but there wasn't any proof that they were involved. There is something else you should know regarding this case and my identity. There are some people around who won't like the fact that I'm a Gulardi, so keeping it quiet as long as possible, might be smart."

"Could this have any connection with the trouble that happened here recently?" Ron asked.

"Rumor has it that the place that blew up and the factory both belonged to the Gulardi's before they died.

"Well, well," Ron said, "that's one more thing we'll have to check on. Now, how about a bank. Do you know anything about the banks they may have used?"

"As far as I know, the U.S. Bank is the only one they ever used. I have a friend who used to work for the Gulardi's helping me track down some of this information as we speak."

"Good," Ron said, "How about bringing him with you tomorrow to the hospital around nine, and we'll get this show on the road."

"We'll be there Ron, and thank you so much."

The men shook hands and Jessie left the office. When he returned to his car, he called Francine.

"Honey," Jessie said, "I just wanted to let you know that I really like Bob's choice in attorneys. Ron Henderson seems to be an alright guy, and he's taking the case. Things will start tomorrow morning when we meet at the hospital. I want you to know that I'm being careful, and with you there, I know you're being careful too. It will seem strange to sleep without you, but thank God, it won't be for too long."

"I told Uncle Bob who you might be, and he said it could be very possible. He had seen your grandfather and your father years ago but never connected the resemblance between you and them. He also said to watch your back because if you are a Gulardi, not all those who embrace you are your friends."

"Honey, that possibility has already been taken into consideration. That's why I have Shooter and a couple more guys watching out for me. Don't worry. I won't be alone in this search."

"Good," Francine said, "I just want you safe and want you back with me. In fact, I think I'll give it about one week, and after that, I'm planning to be wherever you are, so consider yourself warned."

Jessie laughed and said, "OK Honey, one week it is, although I'm hoping it will be sooner. In the meantime, please know I'm thinking about you and can't wait to put my arms around you again. I'll call you tomorrow. Goodnight my sweet."

The next morning Jessie and Shooter met. Shooter had good news for Jessie.

"Last night I made a few calls," Shooter said, "and one was to Bill Tighe. Bill's dad was with your father when they both got shot. At that time, Bill was a runner for the Pesticide business. He said you should call him whenever you need good men. I could have gotten a couple dozen for you already. Everyone I talked to wants you to be the once lost, Gulardi child."

"It makes me feel good that the family was so well liked. Shooter, if possible, I'd like you to go with me to the hospital and meet the attorney I hired yesterday. He wants to talk to you if we can prove my Gulardi ties. We may get answers pretty fast if the hospital can check the prints on the birth certificate to mine." Shooter agreed without hesitation to go with Jessie.

"Leave your car here, Shooter," Jessie said, "and we'll go in mine."

"When do you want the men and where? All I have to do is call," Shooter asked.

"As long as they're available, let's put them to work. How many are there right now Shooter?"

"There are three now and two more due here tomorrow," Shooter said.

"Good," Jessie said, "Have them find out everything they can about Scott. Remember he was the enforcer for the old group? Tell your guys that we want all the information they can dig up on what's going on with him and his group."

Shooter was really pumped. He had always liked Jessie, and it was good to be working for the Gulardi that he believed Jessie to be. Not only that, but it felt good to be back into some action again. He responded with, "You got it boss!" He was soon relaying the message that Jessie had given him. Before hanging up he said, "Be at Sal's at eight tomorrow morning. I'll see you then." With that little chore finished, he turned to Jessie and said, "Why the sudden interest in Scott?"

"Rumor has it that he's trying to reorganize some of his people and pick up where the brothers left off. He's a real bad dude and putting him out of business would do this town a lot of good. Taking him out would be a real privilege for the guy that does that job."

About the time that conversation was finished, they were pulling into the parking lot at the hospital. Once inside, Jessie spotted his new attorney and introduced him to Shooter.

"I just want you to know I've already started earning my money," Ron said. "I contacted the U.S. Bank, and they said Raymond Gulardi not only has a large account but it's still active. Once a year the bank withdraws an amount to cover the cost of the safety deposit box per his written instructions that stays in effect for three more years for a total of twenty-five.

"In addition to the bank info, I also checked here at the hospital and they said that there was a baby born here a little over twenty years ago by the name of Raymond Gulardi III. The birth certificate has two footprints on the back so they'll take a print of your feet and send them both off for comparison. The hospital can tell us if they think they look the same, but the Government has to verify an absolute match."

Jessie was already moving forward when Ron said, "Shall we go in?"

Once inside, Ron led the way to the Records Department where the hospital director was seated at a desk with a file folder in front of him. The Director said, "Your attorney, Mr. Henderson, has acquired the necessary legal paperwork for acquiring a copy of the stated birth certificate. We have made a photocopy for you, Mr. Ruben so all that's required now is for Mr. Henderson to sign the release form."

Once Ron signed the release, he handed the certificate to Jessie and said, "Looks like I was wrong Jessie, there's only one footprint, and that's of the left foot."

The Director said, "Mr. Ruben, if you will have a seat and remove your left shoe and sock, my assistant will take a print of your foot. Once this has been done, we'll sign a certificate that it has been done by us and witnessed by your attorney. You will then send both the copy of the birth certificate print and this print to the government for verification that they are one and the same."

Once the print of Jessie's left foot had been taken, he could hardly contain himself and asked the Director if he thought they appeared to be the same. Both the Director and his assistant looked closely at both prints and said they appeared to be quite close, but only a print expert with proper equipment could verify it for sure.

Jessie said, "Mr. Craft, please accept my thanks to you and your staff for all your help."

Mr. Craft responded with, "You're very welcome Mr. Ruben. This situation is most unusual, but I sincerely hope it works out for you. Now if you'll please excuse me, it's time to get back to the more 'usual' aspects of my job."

"Thanks again," Jessie said.

As Jessie, Shooter and Ron Henderson walked out of the hospital and back to the car, Ron said, "We need to FedEx this overnight and hope for a fast decision."

While they had been walking, Jessie was already on his phone, and they heard him say, "OK, Attention Mr. Shawn and you'll handle the rest? Thanks, I'll handle the other, no charge. Goodbye."

Jessie then directed his attention to Ron and said, "In order to get the verification done a little faster, we'll need to write Attention: Mr. Shawn near the lower left corner of the envelope. The prints will go directly to him and not be lost on someone's desk for a week. It's important because he's the print expert. Ron, I have another job for you, if the Government verifies that the prints are mine, we'll have to do some name changing; from Jessie Ruben back to Raymond Gulardi III."

"By the time we know for sure, I'll have the paperwork completed, and the rest will be a mere formality. I'll also get a court order for the bank. Why don't we all go back to my office for some coffee so I can get some of the family history from Shooter?"

Shooter's voice was shaking a little when he said, "Only if you have something stronger than coffee because I feel like my nerves are jumping out of my skin! I can't believe this is all happening. Never in my wildest dreams does this seem possible1"

"As it turns out, a good attorney is always prepared for such an emergency."

Once they were all seated in Ron's office, each with a drink in hand, Shooter began to relate the history he knew regarding the Gulardi take-over.

"When the Brothers took over," began Shooter, "they had what they called an Unbreakable Lease for all the properties. The dummy corporation was, as they said, set up by Mr. Gulardi to protect his family in case of accident which now supposedly put them in charge. Next, they brought in their crew to replace any of the Gulardi loyal employees. With their power, no one dared to question what they did; plus the fact that so many were receiving payoffs.

"Gradually they got rid of most of the buildings except for the warehouse, which they leased to the head Honcho and of course, retained the business."

Ron said, "OK, then we'll check on all the properties and with the manager that's still left at the factory. Once we get word back on Jessie's I.D., I'll have all the paperwork ready and our first stop will be the bank and the safety deposit box; but in the meantime, all we can do is wait. Jessie, either of us might get the verification back so let's plan to call so we can get together. Please excuse me for a minute; I want to make a copy of those prints for you."

With the original prints sealed in the envelope and the copy in Jessie's pocket, Ron said, "The original is ready to go so you can drop it off now, or I'll do it later."

"We can send them Ron. The FedEx office is right on our way."

"Good," Ron said. "Now we wait."

Jessie and Shooter left Ron's office and headed for the FedEx office. Jessie made sure that the envelope would ship out for "next day" delivery and was soon back in the car heading for the Lake property.

As they got close, Jessie asked, "Shooter, what was the finding on that explosion at the house?"

Shooter said, "The Fire Marshall said that there was a gas leak in the basement, and evidently someone lit a match and 'Boom'! By the way Jessie, what do you have in mind for this place?"

"Right now I'm not real sure," Jessie said, "but there are some thoughts going through my mind. Still Shooter, since you're my man in charge, you should also have some ideas which would include the factory buildings since they're also in the mix."

As they drove through the gate, it brought back memories for Jessie of that fateful night, but he had no regrets since he knew that only two-legged animals had been killed.

"What do you think about rebuilding in the same place Shooter?"

"I think you would have a beautiful home," Shooter said.

"Yes Shooter, it would be a great place for a beautiful home, but not for me. When this is over, my bride and I are out of here!"

"Jessie, you are full of surprises," Shooter said. "Don't tell me you were lucky enough to marry Sal's daughter?"

Jessie laughed and said, "Yes Shooter, Francine and I got married about a week ago in Las Vegas, but we're trying to keep it quiet until we leave so she'll be safe considering the Gulardi name situation." Shooter nodded his agreement as Jessie pulled to a stop close to where the house had been.

"Boy, this place is a real mess!" Jessie said, as he looked around at all the rubble caused from the explosion. "Shooter, this will have to be one of our first jobs so can you arrange for a contractor to clean up this mess next week?" Shooter once again nodded in agreement as he was still a little overwhelmed with everything that was going on.

Jessie said, "I'm going to be gone for a couple days, and I'd like you and your guys to find out all you can about Scott. Such as where he lives, where he hangs out, and how big he's getting to be. Once he finds out who I am, all hell could break loose, and he'll have lost his edge. Hey Shooter, want to have some lunch at Sal's place?"

"I am a little hungry," Shooter said, "so that sounds like a good idea. By the way, will you be calling me while you're gone?"

"Yes Shooter I plan to call you tomorrow night around seven, if that's OK."

"Seven sounds like a good number. Hopefully we'll have some news for you regarding Scott and his crew."

"One more place you could check is Tony's Restaurant and Bar. That used to be one of the meeting places," Jessie said.

The drive to Sal's took only a short time. Once they were seated, had their coffee in front of them, and their food ordered, they were able to discuss some of Jessie's plans.

"Shooter, once I get my name back," Jessie said, "I hope that I can leave this town better than when I came here with the Gulardi name remembered with honesty and respect like it used to be. In the meantime, let's keep in touch. I'll be calling you on a regular basis, and of course, you can call me anytime as well. Perhaps you can locate a good housing contractor that we can meet with regarding re-building the lake property."

When Jessie and Shooter had finished their meal, Jessie said, "Well, I guess I'd better take off now so I'm leaving it all in your capable hands. Oh, by the way, how are you fixed for money?"

"I'm in good shape Jessie," Shooter said, "You made sure of that."

"Great, but whatever you spend, let me know, and I'll reimburse you."

Once Jessie left Sal's place, he got in his car and called Francine. "Honey, put some clothes in a bag, enough for a few days, and I'll pick you up in a few minutes."

Thirty minutes later, with Francine in the car, they began their drive to Atlantic City, New Jersey with two nights spent in motels along the way. They made love at every opportunity and even pulled off the main road a couple times, laughing like teenagers pulling the wool over someone's eyes. Of course the idea that they might get caught only added to their passion and excitement. Each realized that everything they did was making memories and strengthening the deep love they felt for each other.

Francine asked Jessie about the few days they had been separated. He told her about the trip to the hospital to retrieve a copy of his birth certificate. Jessie explained about having been "foot printed" and laughed at how funny it sounded. He told her that a copy had been sent to Washington for final analysis and comparison. He said, "We should get an answer back in a couple days, but I brought a copy for you to look at."

Francine looked at the print and could see a couple lines here and there, which appeared to be in approximately the same place on both, but was unable to tell for sure if they were a match.

"Don't feel bad about it honey," Jessie said, "That's why the print had to be sent to Washington for the print experts to analyze. They use equipment with very high magnification and compare them line by line until they're sure they either match or don't match. We'll know soon."

The couple days had flown by quickly. They were on the outskirts of New Jersey when Jessie's cell phone rang and startled them both. Jessie answered and was not surprised that it was Ron calling.

"Jessie," Ron said, "I just got a special delivery envelope and wondered when you'd be here so we can open it together."

"Right now I'm about forty miles from there," Jessie said, "so give me about an hour and I'll be there."

"That was an important call, am I right?" Francine asked.

"Yes honey, our answer came back," Jessie said, "and he's waiting for me to open it. When I find out, you'll be the first one I'll call."

Jessie dropped Francine off at her Aunt's house and drove to Ron's office. Jessie was usually pretty cool about most things, but he felt a great deal of anxiety on this drive to his attorney's office. His foot was a little heavy on the pedal, and he beat his one-hour estimate by fifteen minutes and was soon parked at Ron's office. When Jessie walked in, Ron was at his desk and waved him in.

Jessie said, "Traffic was light so I made good time, Ron. I only hope it's worth it."

"One way to find out Jessie," Ron said, "Here it is. You do the honors."

Jessie took the envelope from Ron's hand, tore the seal, removed the paper, and started to read. He actually read the document several times over, allowing its information to sink in and finally said, "Ron, it looks like we can get that court order for the bank. Raymond Gulardi III has come home!"

Jessie handed the document to Ron. After he read it, he said, "You're right, the Government has confirmed your identity." Ron stood up, put his hand out to shake the hand of the man across his desk, and said, "Glad to know you, Ray. Now my work really begins. There's a good chance I can get this order signed today, but if not, first thing tomorrow morning. I'll give you a call as soon as it's done."

Ron made a copy of the document for Jessie. As he left the attorney's office, he knew that from this moment forward, Jessie Ruben would cease to exist as he took his rightful place as Raymond Gulardi III. He had loved his adoptive parents dearly, but they had given him their final gift of love by giving him the information of his true identity.

Chapter 36

When Ray got to his car, his first call was to his beautiful bride Francine. When she answered, he said, "Hello Honey, or should I call you Mrs. Raymond Gulardi III?"

Francine squealed with excitement on the phone and said "Oh Jessie, I mean Ray. Oh Honey, that's just wonderful news! How do you feel about it all? What's going to happen now?"

"Well honey, I guess that means we'll have to get married again with the new name of Gulardi so everything will be legal. I have to know you'll be safe so stay with your aunt for awhile longer. I love you honey, but there's much more to be done so I'll talk to you later. Bye for now."

Ray then called Shooter and said, "Well Shooter, the word came back. I am, in fact, Raymond Gulardi III. I wanted you to know that we may go to the bank tomorrow once Ron gets the order signed. I'd like you to meet me at eight in the morning at Sal's place and have a man with you. Tell the other guys to keep an eye on Scott."

"Will do," Shooter said, "and I think you'll like what we've found out so far. Tomorrow I'll bring Jocko with me 'cause nobody screws with him. I've also found a clean-up guy who said that a full day's work at the lake property would make it so you won't know the place. Maybe we can meet him later tomorrow afternoon? Boss, I have another question. While you're here, why don't you stay at my place? I have plenty of room. We could watch your back a lot easier."

"Thanks Shooter, I think that's a great idea. I'd like to do that for a couple days until we see how things look. By tomorrow night, word will be on the street that I'm here so I'll see you in a few."

Armed with Shooter's address, Ray drove to his house. It was a small two-bedroom frame in an older neighborhood. He parked beside Shooter's car and walked to the front door and knocked.

"Come in, the doors open," the voice said.

When Ray walked in, he saw two men sitting on the couch drinking beer.

"Pull up a chair boss, how about a cold one?" Shooter said. "This is Jocko, and he'll be coming with us tomorrow. This is Rip. He'll be with the guys watching Scott."

Ray shook hands with both men and noticed that Jocko was of medium build with black hair and eyes to match, weighed about one eighty and about six feet tall. Rip, on the other hand, was much bigger, probably weighed 250 and stood about three inches taller than Jocko with dark hair and blue eyes. Ray was pleased with the firm handshake from them both and happy that they were on his side as he could tell they could be formidable adversaries.

"I'm glad to know you," Jocko said. "Your dad was a good man, and the bastards that killed your family are now dead and good riddance. What you got in mind for us to do?"

"If it's still mine, I want to rebuild the old house as soon as we can. Shooter will take over here, including the factory. He needs people around him that he can trust. Once Scott and his crew are put down, I'll be leaving for an extended period of time, although I may eventually come back."

"Scott has about thirty guys working for him," Shooter said, "and they've been busting heads and shaking down all the people they can. He's not into the dope yet but will be before long. Word is...he's looking for a supplier. They have a house off Highway 130 where Scott lives. They sometimes meet at Tony's Bar and Grill."

"Is he married or does he live alone?" Ray asked.

"No wife," Shooter said, "but sometimes a girlfriend. He had a war meeting with his two top lieutenants. They got a lot of people scared in a very short time since they started trying to take over. If the A.T.F. could have gotten him, this town would have been better off. Even the honest cops couldn't find a witness against him."

Before Ray could say anything, his cell rang. It was Ron.

"Good news," Ron said, "Klein is the name of the judge that signed the order, and he remembered your father. He said that when he was a young attorney, he worked for him once on a land title deal. He said he's glad you're safe and asked that you come by to see him sometime. The bank opens at nine, so we can meet there if that's alright."

"That'll work just fine Ron. We'll see you tomorrow at nine."

As Ray turned off the phone, Shooter said, "So, what's our plan for tomorrow?"

"Shooter," Ray said, "You and I will go to the bank in one car. Jocko will stay behind us to watch who comes into the bank. When we leave, he'll check to see if we're followed; and if not, we'll all meet back at your place. Then we'll go see that contractor about the clean up and go by Scott's place on the way back here. Once we get back here, we can discuss additional moves and plans."

The four men all felt comfortable with each other, and the plans that would soon unfold when one of them mentioned having hunger pangs.

Shooter said, "I know just the place, it's a homey pub about a mile from here. Come on guys, I'll drive." They all piled into Shooter's car and drove to the pub. It was a quaint little place with a bar, a few tables and a jute box. After a few beers, some sandwiches and hot chicken wings, they headed back to Shooter's place. Jocko and Rip left in their cars. Shooter showed Ray his room.

Perhaps it was the relief of finding his new identity or even the relaxation the beer had given him, but whatever the reason, Ray slept deep and peaceful. He woke up only when Jocko's car pulled up to the house at seven the next morning. He grabbed a quick shower and soon joined Shooter and Jocko for a cup of morning coffee.

"How about breakfast at Mom and Dad's eatery? Ray said. "They used to have a good meal before it was sold. I'd bet it's just about as good now." They all agreed.

They left Shooter's house with Ray and Shooter in one car and Jocko driving his own. Once they arrived at the restaurant, they were shown to a booth and ordered coffee. It didn't take long to decide on their breakfast. The new chef was pretty fast, and it wasn't long before their food was brought to the table. The conversation stopped as the three men ate. Once they had consumed most of their breakfast, Ray said, "Those were real homemade biscuits, so looks like I was right about the food being as good as before!"

They all ordered a second cup of coffee and Ray said, "This is where we separate. Jocko, you know where the bank is so when you're ready, you leave first and find a place to park where you can see the area around the bank entrance. You'll be able to see us go in and anyone else that might follow us in or be hanging around outside." The plans were made and agreed upon. Ray and Shooter watched Jocko drive away from the restaurant and followed a few minutes later.

Ron was waiting in the parking lot when they arrived and the three entered the bank together. Ron led the way to the bank's president, and as Mr. Johnson looked up, Ron laid the court order on his desk.

Mr. Johnson said, "I see Judge Klein signed the order. This is all I need. Gentlemen, please have a seat while I retrieve the books."

Ron, Ray, and Shooter pulled up chairs near Mr. Johnson's desk and waited for his return from the vault. Their wait was brief. Mr. Johnson soon returned with a large ledger, placed it on his desk, and began studying the pages.

"I'm sorry I'm so slow," Mr. Johnson said, "but I'm not familiar with the Gulardi records as they were before my time. Yes, here we are, Box 2121. If you will follow me Mr. Gulardi, we can go get the safety deposit box."

Ray followed Mr. Johnson to the vault area where the lock box was opened and the safety deposit box removed. Mr. Johnson showed Ray to a private room where he could review the contents unobserved. Feeling a chill as he opened the lid, Ray paused for a moment. When the chill had passed, he looked in.

On top were some pictures that Ray noticed had been marked with names and dates on the backs and decided to study them later. Under the pictures was a large envelope that contained some deeds and under the envelope was a large ledger. When Ray lifted the ledger, he found that the bottom of the box was lined with bundles of hundred-dollar bills and below them was another slim envelope that held treasury bonds. Ray called the banker back in and asked him to take care of the money and the bonds while he returned to the other men.

When he returned to Mr. Johnson's office, he gave Ron the deeds and began looking through the pictures. The first picture was of his Grandfather and Grandmother. The next picture was his father and mother and a young girl. In the picture, his mother was obviously pregnant. As he looked at the names, he realized the small girl had been his sister and that meant he was the next to be born. As he gazed upon the face of the mother he had never known, he realized she had been pregnant with him when the picture was taken. He was so deep in thought that he never saw the banker return.

"Mr. Gulardi," the banker said, "That is a very substantial amount of money. What do you want us to do with it?"

Ray said, "Open an account for Gulardi Enterprises. This, pointing to Shooter, is the Vice President, and my lawyer, if he will agree, is on the Board of Directors. He'll have the papers drawn up."

"There is also another account in your father's name," Mr. Johnson said, "How shall we handle that?"

Ray said, "Please add my name and remove my father's name. Where are the statements mailed to?"

"The statements were never mailed," Mr. Johnson, said. "Your father didn't want any so the account remained open by the safety deposit box rent. I don't know if you realize how wealthy you are, Mr. Gulardi."

"Thank you Mr. Johnson," Ray said. "If you will handle setting up those accounts, we can sign the paperwork before we leave. Ron will get whatever papers you need so we can get to work."

When Mr. Johnson left to get the signature cards, Ron said, "There are more than just the two places here. From what I can see, there is over fifty acres across from the lake property on the other side of the road that is also yours."

Ray said, "There are two homes on that land."

"Then we need a survey to find out what's what," Ron said, "and I want to get a copy of these and leave the originals here."

"Sounds like a plan, Ron," Ray said, "but here's a ledger you may understand better than I can, so please see what you think."

About then the banker returned with the papers to be signed. Once all the signatures had been completed, Ray said, "We'll be back tomorrow to go through everything we've talked about today and tie up any loose ends."

"Everything will be ready whenever you arrive." Ray thanked him and the three began walking toward the door.

"Damn," Ray said, "I never called Jocko." Ray dialed his number and told him they were through with the banking business and would meet him at Sal's for lunch at twelve noon.

Everything was going according to plan. Ron would be getting all the forms prepared along with a visit to the Registrar's office. He told Ray to meet him at his office the following morning to get all the paperwork completed for the enterprise they were starting. Ray and Shooter headed out to the lake property to meet with the contractor about the cleanup and to check out the property across the road. As they drove by the gate, they stopped and looked at the two houses. The two homes were mirror images of each other, except for the paint color, with the garages in the middle and the main entrances to the outside—making the two residences completely private from one another. Ray thought about the house that had been blown up and suddenly realized that the lake house was very similar to these two. He told Shooter that he thought the same contractor had built all three.

"Well boss, looks like you'll have two more rentals to worry about." Shooter said.

Ray laughed and said, "I got news for you Shooter. Taking care of rentals is part of the new manager's job so looks like **you've** got two more rentals to take care of, as well as the machine business!" Shooter laughed too but was extremely pleased that Ray trusted him enough to take responsibility for all that was being handed to him.

They drove through the gate at the lake property where the clean-up contractor was waiting for them. Ray told Shooter to make the arrangements for the cleanup while he took a walk toward the lake.

Ray was deep in thought about all that had been put on his own plate. He thought about the death of his adoptive parents, discovering his true identity, and all the responsibility that came with it. How very fortunate he was to have his Francine. He was indeed, a very lucky man. Finally he let his mind and his eyes take in the beauty of the beautiful lake and its surroundings.

He was brought out of his reverie by the sound of Shooter's voice calling his name.

Ray walked back to the car. Shooter told him that all the arrangements for the clean up had been completed and explained the price and the details. Ray was in agreement with everything and said, "Let's drive by Scott's place, and then you can call your crew and see if they have any news for us."

Luck was on their side as this was an old neighborhood where the homes had very large yards and the only streetlight was almost a block away in either direction. The small frame house was set back toward the rear of the property, as were the others on the same block. Each home appeared to be approximately the same distance apart. They drove to the corner and drove behind the homes, passing an alley in the process.

"Let's take off Shooter," Ray said. "I've seen all I need to. Scott's house is plain. When more money rolls in, he'll move to a fancier place so he's not there yet."

Chapter 37

When they arrived back at Shooter's place and walked in, they were met by Jocko and three middle-aged men.

Shooter said, "Ray, I'd like you to meet Jimbo, Luke and Matt. These are the other three I told you about."

While Ray shook hands with all three men, Shooter brought them all a beer.

"I'm glad you could all make it," Ray said. "The first order of business is to let you know that Shooter is now the manager of Gulardi Enterprises. He'll act on my behalf, as I'll be gone before long. Shooter knows what I want and what needs to be done. The second order of business regards Scott and his crew. Scott is a very dangerous individual and so are his two head men. Once they're out of the picture, the others will probably scatter so your jobs are to look after Shooter until we know that any danger has passed. Does anyone have any information on Scott or his crew?"

"Most of the gambling," Luke said, "and whore houses are starting to pay off. They've got everybody scared. We hear there's a couple cops on his payroll so nobody stops his crew from intimidating anyone they want to intimidate. The words out that he's planning to take a trip, probably to find a supplier for the dope. Since the D.E.A and A.T.F came in and cleaned up, the suppliers are being pretty careful who they deal with."

"That's a little bit of good news," Ray said. "Now I'll let Shooter fill you in on the plans while I go make a couple phone calls." With that, Ray left the room as Shooter continued to explain the plans for the future.

Ray called Francine and said, "Hello Love of my Life. I just wanted to let you know that I'll see you tomorrow. We need to take a couple days off. I've got a lot to talk to you about, and we'll need to make some plans." Francine was excited and wanted Ray to tell her everything on the phone, but he teased her by telling her she'd have to wait until they got together. After words of love between the two, they hung up with Ray telling her that he'd see her around four p.m. the following afternoon.

Once the call to Francine was completed, he called Ron and said, "Good evening Ron. I hope I didn't disturb you."

"Not at all," Ron said, "In fact, I was about to call you. Everything came out like we expected. You definitely own the lake property as well as the land and homes across the street. Your grandfather lived in the lake house and some other members of the Gulardi family lived in the other two houses. The rent checks, taxes and all correspondence are sent to the warehouse office at the plant. I had a chance to talk with the office manager and told her you'd see her tomorrow. I filed your name change and recorded everything in Gulardi Enterprises. Does that sound alright to you?"

"That all sounds great, Ron," Ray said. "And the next thing regards my wife. I'm pretty sure of what will need to be done but I'd like your input on the details. Since we were married with the name of Ruben, what legal action do you think we should take at this point?"

"Well," Ron said, "I think the simple way would be to have your first marriage annulled, and then remarry under your real name of Gulardi."

"That's what I thought but wanted to check with you first. When you file the papers for licensing for the Corporation, I'd like to include my wife's name, Francine."

Ron responded with "No problem Ray. I'll take care of that and please have Shooter call me so I can get his full legal name for the paperwork as well. We'll all be shown as company officers like you've specified. I'll send a copy for you to the plant office."

Ray was pleased with Ron's skill at getting things accomplished and said, "Great Ron. It sounds like you have everything under control so keep in touch if necessary but otherwise, call Shooter as he has my authority."

When Ray hung up, he went into the living room with the guys and said, "Shooter, for the next few days, I want you guys to keep a very close eye on Scott. I want to know what time he goes to bed, what time he gets up, and how he spends every minute of his day. Set up the shifts that will work best, but the main thing is not to be seen so he won't be tipped off. What we need is to spot any weakness, and then we can make plans accordingly."

Jocko said, "Why not just take him out? Hell, I'll do the job for free!"

Ray responded with, "No, I want you boys to stay clean unless things change. We have no other choice. My family made big money in this town, and from what I've heard, never hurt anyone. I believe we can do the same since we already have the resources to accomplish that."

By the time the other guys had left, two hours had gone by, leaving Shooter and Ray alone.

"Do you rent this place, or is it yours?" Ray asked.

"It's just a rental," Shooter said, "because I stayed at the lake most of the time."

"Good," Ray said. "As soon as the lake house is rebuilt, I'd like you to live there, rent free of course, as one of your perks for handling our businesses. Tomorrow we need to meet with Ron at the bank and get some of the finer details for the business set up including a checkbook for your use and a credit card for me. I don't want any statements unless I call for them for some reason. No sense having a bunch of extra paperwork around for unauthorized people to get their hands on."

It was late so they decided to call it a night.

The following morning they met Ron at the bank, and the paperwork and instructions were completed. Ray had just asked Ron to have the credit card mailed to the office when Shooter's cell phone rang.

"It's me Shooter," Rocko said. "I'm following one of Scott's men, and he's right down the street from the bank. He seems to be watching to see who comes out."

"Is he alone Jocko or is someone else with him?" Shooter asked.

"He's alone but it looks like he's holding a camera. What does Ray want me to do?"

"I'll put Ray on the phone, and you can tell him what you told me," Shooter said.

Ray listened as Jocko explained and then said, "Nothing, just keep your eyes open. We're getting ready to come out now. See what he does, and if he follows us, give me a call. While I have you on the phone, we'll be headed for the factory office to see the office manager there."

When Ray finished the call, he handed the phone back to Shooter and thanked the banker for his help.

"Come on Shooter. Let's not keep the man with the camera waiting," Ray said. "I wonder what took so long for them to find out to see who I am."

As they left the bank, they checked both ways and saw the car about half a block away with what appeared to be a camera pointing at them. Unable to resist, Ray gave him a one-finger salute before getting into Shooter's car.

"Well Shooter," Ray said, "It looks like the game is on. Scott is bound to recognize me in that photo, and I sure wish I could be a fly on the wall to hear what he has to say about it all. I'd bet the air would be blue! Anyway, let's head for the plant and see if he follows."

When Ray looked in the rearview mirror, he saw that the car was still in the same spot and not following them so he said, "Damn, we have to meet the contractor at ten so head for the lake, and we'll go to the plant after that." No sooner had the words left his mouth when Shooter's cell rang. He handed it over to Ray.

"Hello Jocko, what's happening?"

"Well, it looks like we're headed back to Scott's place so I'll stay with him."

"OK Jocko. We're headed to the lake property to meet with a contractor, and then we'll be going to the plant after that. From there, we'll head for Shooter's place." As the call ended, Shooter was headed for the contractor's office.

When they went inside, Ray told the receptionist that they had an appointment to meet with Mr. Jamish.

"Yes sir, he's expecting you. Please go right in."

As they entered the office, an older man rose to greet them and shook hands first with Shooter and then with Ray. As he shook Ray's hand, he said, "Son, you look a lot like your father. He was the one that requested those homes be built."

"Thank you Mr. Jamish," Ray said. "We were wondering who built them."

"My father and I built them back when we were just starting out in business," Mr. Jamish responded. "Your father gave us the opportunity to build those three homes and that made a great beginning for our business. We were grateful for the faith he had in us as a new company. Your father wanted some consistency in the two places across from the lake so we decided to build mirror image homes which are much the same but so different. He loved them with their similarities but appreciated their differences. Your father had the lake house built for your grandparents to live in."

"We'd like you to rebuild the house on the lake," Ray said. "What we have in mind is a four-bedroom ranch with full basement, three-car attached garage, with full windows facing the lake. Is it possible for us to look at some plans?"

"Yes, it is absolutely possible. In fact, we've just built four homes on the other side of town. Look at them and make any changes you might want. We'll get started when you give the word."

After looking over the various floor plans, making requested minor changes and the price agreed upon, Ray told him he was free to start building at the lake as soon as possible.

From the lake, they drove to the plant office to see the manager.

"The last time I was here was to make a delivery to that building over there," Ray said. "Now I'm back as the owner. Funny how life runs in a circle."

As they walked into the small office, they saw the manager Gene Riker sitting at his desk. He looked up and said, "May I help you?"

"Yes, my name is Raymond Gulardi, the new owner. My attorney, Ron Henderson has all the necessary paperwork so we came out to meet you and see what your needs might be. This is Mr. Ken Walls, or Shooter, as we call him. He'll be running Gulardi Enterprises, which is the new name for the prior organization. As of now, there are no major changes in store although we do hope to increase the machine business and perhaps add something else in time.

"Ron will tell you where to send any monies due the company. We'll be using the same bank that you've been using although the former account has been frozen by the judge. You can call Mr. Johnson at the bank to find out the details. If there's anything you need, Shooter will be available to assist you. One more thing, if any mail comes for us, please hold on to it until we see you."

"I'll do that," Gene said. "It just came to me that it was your family that started this business, then sold it to the brothers."

"No, that's what they were telling everyone," Ray said. "The truth is, they never bought it, stolen is a better word. That's why the judge seized their bank account, and it'll be turned over to Gulardi Enterprises. Any money needed for payroll or expenses, ask Shooter. We've got to get going now as I have another appointment. Nice meeting you Gene."

Back on the road, Ray told Shooter he had a trip to take, but he'd be back in two days.

"I'd like you to come back here to make sure they get the payroll out and take care of any invoices that need to be paid. Keep Rocko and a couple men on Scott and his crew. Keep one man with you at all times, Shooter, just in case. I believe Scott will wait to see what I have in mind. Right now, no one knows our strength. He may want to talk to me before he makes a move."

Right then, Ray's cell phone rang, and it was Ron.

"I wanted you to know that Judge Klein is hearing our motions," Ron said. "By tomorrow, the bank business will be settled. Do you want it all in the Gulardi Enterprise account?"

"Yes," Ray said. "That's the only one we'll use, and if need be, I'll add to it. As soon as you get time Ron, please go down to the plant office and get the licenses and tax form in our new name. Anything else that needs to be changed, please take care of it. I'll be gone for a couple days, but Shooter will be here if you need him. You can also get in touch with me by phone if necessary."

"Tell Shooter I have court in the morning but should be at the office by one o'clock. Have him meet me there so he can sign the applications," Ron said.

Once the call ended, Ray told Shooter what had been discussed.

"Boss, that's already more money than I've ever seen so I hope I can measure up to your expectations," Shooter said.

"Shooter," Ray said, "When I'm not around, run any questions or worries by Ron. He's our attorney, and I have him on a retainer, so don't think you're ever alone. Even when I'm gone from here, I'll still keep in touch with you and Ron. Besides, you'll do just fine."

Chapter 38

Back at Shooter's, Ray got his own car and left to pick up Francine. Once alone in the car, he called the Virginia number and made himself known to his contact.

"Hello Ray, glad you called. I hear so far it's all good news. How can I help you?"

"My wife and I will be at Trump Towers in Atlantic City for two nights. I still drive the same blue Buick, and my trunk will be unlocked. What I want is two remotes, set up with magnetos for cars. Scott has a dope contact, but I don't know about gun running yet. My man here says he knew the whole operation so it's just a matter of time until he trades guns for dope. The profits will skyrocket, as the guns are cheap. Funny how both sides think they're cheating the other. My next call will be in a couple weeks, so have a good weekend."

Ray had never been much of an outwardly emotional person. He had loved his adoptive parents and the passing of his father was the closest he had ever come to showing extreme emotion. It wasn't that he didn't feel things; he just didn't show emotion where others could see. In his line of work, he couldn't allow his feelings to interfere with a job that needed to be done. But when it came to Francine, she was so much a part of him that he could easily allow his love for her to show.

The next three days were all Ray could have asked for. Being away from his Francine for a couple days and then being with her was like having their honeymoon all over again. Not only was she so very beautiful, but she was a warm and loving person as well. He hated every moment when he couldn't be with her.

Now he had to tell her that they would have to be apart for a few more days, and then they'd head back, once again, for the West Coast.

Back in Camden, after numerous goodbye kisses, he let Francine off at her Uncle's house and drove to a local park. Ray opened the trunk of his car and saw that the delivery had been made. Two separate boxes were over the spare tire. Ray called Shooter and told him that there was no way possible he would be there tonight.

"I'll meet you tomorrow morning at Sal's for breakfast."

Ray found a motel out of town and rented a room for one night. He ate a small dinner and returned to his room to watch TV. The hardest part of any job was the waiting.

Around two o'clock, he drove to where Scott lived, found a place to park, and saw only one car there. Taking one of the remotes, he removed the magnetic charge and staying as hidden as possible, made his way to the car. Lying on his back, he placed the charge under the driver's seat. This done, he returned to the motel. Satisfied with his night's work, he felt ready to end another dope dealer's dreams. This message should be loud and clear to whoever was left. A hot shower was all he needed for sleep that night.

Awakening around seven, he got dressed and drove to Sal's to meet Shooter. As he entered, he saw Shooter and Matt at a booth close to the kitchen.

"Glad you got here boss. We've lost Jimbo," Shooter said. "Someone shot him in his car last night or early this morning. Rocko thinks he got careless and was caught by Scott or one of his lieutenants and was shot as a warning to us."

"What do you think Matt?" Ray asked.

"Could be," Matt said, "Jimbo was big but never carried a gun, only muscle. He wasn't a man to have any enemies but was a good one to have on your side."

"Shooter, call all the boys to your house for a meeting tonight," Ray said. I'll meet you there around seven. From now on, everyone packs a piece. Luke needs to pair up with one of you three that's left. That way, one watches the other's back. We too, can play hardball when it's pushed on us. What are your plans for today, Shooter?"

"When we leave here, I'm heading to the lake to see how the cleanup is going. From there to the plant to see about a clean up of the whole place. There's a lot of space not being used that could be rented until we need it. How about you boss? How can we play it safe and not you?"

"I'll be OK," Ray, said, "I'm going to see Ron before I go see Judge Klein. Don't worry about me; there are too many people around."

Breakfast for the three was soon over so they all left at the same time.

Ray drove to a public park where he could be alone and backed into a remote spot, opened the back door, and removed the rear seat. Looking down, he could see the bonds stacked neatly with a sniper rifle in the middle. At the other end was a 9 mm pistol with a silencer. This was the last of his arsenal. He removed the pistol and replaced the seat. Before putting the gun in its holster, he checked the clip to make sure it was fully loaded. Satisfied, he resumed his trip to see Ron. There in the parking lot was a car that looked familiar. Damn, if that's not the car from Scott's house. Going on by, Ray parked about one block away and watched who came out of Ron's office. He wasn't surprised to see Scott and one other man come out. When they drove away and were out of sight, he drove to the lot and parked. As he entered the office, the secretary told him that Ron was expecting him and to go right in.

"Hello Ray," Ron said, "I'm glad you're a little late. I just had a visitor asking about you."

"Oh," Ray said, "Now who could that be?"

"Sounds like you may have seen him," Ron said.

"I did," Ray said, "and parked out of sight until they left. Who was the other guy with him?"

"Said his name was Art Genns," Ron said. "Didn't talk much, just one mean guy. Not one to mess with as he had a gun in his shoulder holster. Both said you looked familiar to them and wanted to know what your name was before. I told them I had no idea, as you never said."

"Thanks for that," Ray said. "It's none of their business who I was. Maybe they saw someone that looked like me. My purpose for seeing you today is to find out if there's anything you need me to sign today before I leave."

"No, I got the tax number yesterday and visited the plant office. The money from the Uterio account was transferred to your Enterprise Company. We'll file the Corporation papers tomorrow, if Shooter's available. One more thing Ray, watch your ass out there. That twosome spelled trouble. That Scott fellow was investigated when all that shit hit the fan, but there were no witnesses, no evidence so they had to turn him loose."

"Sometimes when you come through what he did," Ray said, "he probably feels lucky like he's got a horseshoe up his ass. The trouble is that luck only lasts so long. Do you think Judge Klein is in his office? I'd like to see him before I leave town."

"Until eleven," Ron said, "then it's court until one o'clock and then he goes home."

"Thanks again. You take care of yourself and please look after Shooter for me. I'll be in touch."

The courthouse was Ray's next stop and only a short drive from Ron's office. He parked behind the courthouse and went inside through a side door. He headed to the lobby and found the office directory, located the judge's office on the second floor, room 233, and caught the elevator up. As he entered the office, a secretary asked if he had an appointment.

"No ma'am, my name is Raymond Gulardi, and I'd like to see Judge Klein," Ray said.

"Please have a seat," the secretary said, "I'll find out if he has any time available."

Ray sat down and watched as she called the judge on the intercom and told him who was waiting to see him. Without hesitation, the judge told her to send him right in. As Ray walked through the door, the judge extended his hand to shake Ray's and said, "My God, you are the spitting image of your grandfather! It's like looking at him without his gray hair!"

"Thank you sir. I needed that," Ray said. "I wanted to talk to you about my family."

"I knew both your Dad and Grandfather. Anything that needed an attorney was handled by me so there were few secrets that I didn't know. When your grandmother died, your mother and father were there. Your mother was carrying you in her arms and that was the last time I saw any of them alive. The next thing I knew, the Uterio Brothers had papers supposedly signed by your grandfather, turning everything over to the new corporation. The documentation showed that your grandfather was the President of the new corporation which had started two months prior so no one smelt a rat."

"Thank you sir, a lot of my questions have now been answered," Ray said. "I guess it's not hard to get a notary to date and log it as that date. By saying he was the President, it looked real to whoever didn't know him.

"I'll be leaving here very soon, but my attorney, Ken Anderson and my new headman, Ken Walls, or Shooter as most know him, will take care of our new company. I know it will be an asset to the community, and God willing, we'll be giving something back if all goes as planned."

They said their good-byes, and Ray left the courthouse to drive by Tony's Bar and Grill on his way back to Shooter's house. There, parked in front, was the car that belonged to Scott and one other vehicle. Ray drove by but decided to wait them out so parked down the block. He opened his glove compartment and took out the remote and thought that perhaps this would be the day he could leave this town. He looked at his watch and saw it was eleven-thirty. This had to be a coffee break, unless it was a meeting. One thing he had learned in the service was how to be patient. You could plan your next move but knew that nothing was guaranteed to go exactly as you planned.

Ray was still troubled about where Scott got enough money to get started because good help was not cheap. Remembering their meetings, he realized there wasn't a lot of brains required, only muscle. Taking a positive mental approach, Ray knew that with Scott out of the way, there would be a lull in the business until a replacement could be found. The town would come out the winner for awhile.

With time on his hands, he called his contact in Virginia to let them know that he would finish his work today. He also told them that he felt that someone else might be calling the shots

"We think the same way," his contact said. "We checked his service record, and it showed us the same thing. Never promoted and only a bad ass bitch discharged with an undesirable. He wasn't able to find a job he was good at until he met a guy he had known before by the name of Romero. It was Romero who gave him the start and opportunity to be himself. No one would testify against him, and at most all he'd get was a short jail term. Any payback from him or any of his men who got away could be real bad.

"There were a few who got away that might know how to step in, and they also made a lot of money for services rendered. Politicians, lawyers and cops were all on the payroll. With the old crew gone, the town was wide-open and easy picking. Funny thing is, with no dope and no guns involved, we wouldn't be interested in the small stuff as the local law would be handle that.

"Drugs support terrorism, and unfortunately, America is the most guilty of the people who buy. Guns are traded for dope which is sold for a high profit, then more guns are bought, and traded for dope—it's a vicious cycle. When you get where you're going, call in, and we'll keep you informed on what we uncover."

Just then, Ray saw four men coming out of Tony's and told his contact goodbye. Ray fingered his remote.

One man went to the passenger side of Scott's car and got in. Another man got in the driver's seat of the other car. Scott and the fourth man walked between the cars, and Scott got in. As the man leaned down toward Scott to tell him something, Ray pushed the button on the remote. Before the sound of the explosion had died, Ray was driving away toward Shooter's place.

Ray was thankful for the key. He went in, grabbed a cold beer, and turned on the television. The program he was watching was interrupted by a breaking story. There had just been an explosion in front of Tony's Bar and Grill. The first report was that there were three dead and one on life support. More news later as facts were made known. He would leave tonight after meeting with his people. He and Francine would return to Las Vegas to get remarried as Gulardi. He decided he'd better call her.

"Hi honey," Ray said, "my business is almost caught up; other than a short meeting tonight, we can head back to the West Coast either late tonight or early tomorrow morning. What's your preference?"

Francine responded in a very sexy, almost purring voice saying, "Perhaps we could stay over for the night and practice up for our next honeymoon." At that, Ray felt more than just his heart jump.

"OK, you sexy little vixen. I'll pick you up after the meeting tonight. Please tell Carol and Bob how much I appreciate you being able to stay with them. Oh, and by the way, I love you."

It was around 6:30 when Shooter pulled into the drive, followed by Luke. Shooter said, "The other two called and said they'd be a little late."

"Well Guys, how was your day?" Ray asked.

"They're cleaning up everything, including the basement," Shooter said. "When they inspected it, they said there was just too much damage for a repair job. It will be cheaper in the long run to start over. Including the cleanup though, they expect to have the house completed in three to four months. I also have some other good news. I've worked out a rent deal with the two contractors to store their equipment at the back of the plant. Luke said he and Matt were both welders so how about us starting a shop? It would give us another business."

"That's why I made you the Man. Remember Ron is our lawyer

and can help you boys all the way. By the way, did you hear about an explosion at Tony's? It just came on the news?"

"Did you say explosion?" Shooter asked. "What happened, or did they say?"

"Something about three dead and the other guy didn't look so good," Ray said. "Maybe someone took out Tony or Tony got even for something. Well guys, think I'll be leaving now. Shooter, everything is in your hands. Before the house is finished, I'll wire more money to Ron so you don't have to worry about it. I'll call on a regular basis, but if there's anything you need, don't hesitate to call me. In the meantime, you guys protect your asses until I see you again. Tell Jocko and Matt I said goodbye."

With the good-byes completed all around, Ray headed for the car to call Francine and let her know he was on his way. He remembered there was a flower shop on the way so decided to stop and get some flowers for Francine and her Aunt. Ray had good taste, and both bouquets were gorgeous. Then he decided to stop by the liquor store and pick up a couple bottles of wine for Bob. With his arms loaded down with flowers and wine, he could only tap the door with his foot. It was Carol who opened the door. Her eyes lit up when she saw the flowers, and Ray told her, "Ones for you and ones for Francine."

"Oh thank you Jessie, oh, I mean Ray, they are so beautiful! Please come in. Francine is upstairs packing her things and should be down in a few minutes."

Ray saw Bob sitting in the other room, went in, and offered him the wine.

"Bob, I picked up this wine for you as a token of my appreciation for you guys watching after Francine while I had all this running around to do. I hope it's something you like, but if not, there's a liquor store a couple blocks down. I can get something else if you'd prefer."

"No need to do more shopping Ray," Bob said. "These are perfect. In fact we enjoy a little glass of wine in the evenings, and this happens to be our choice too. Thanks so much, and believe me, we have truly enjoyed Francine staying here with us. Those two gals get along like two peas in a pod. Mom says you're leaving tonight?"

"Yes," Ray said, "We'll probably drive for a few hours and then get a room and by tomorrow night we'll be in Colorado. Once we get to Vegas, the first thing we're going to do is get married. That guy she married before has left so I'll take his place. Ha-ha."

Bob laughed too and said, "It's been a long time since your family ate at our place and didn't know any of them real well except for your grandfather. I remember your dad came in with him a few times. Finding out who you were let me see the resemblance of you to them, and I don't know why I didn't recognize it before. What I'm trying to say Ray, is that everyone I've talked to is glad to know that you're alive and happy to see that you've returned."

"Maybe someday we'll come back," Ray said, "but right now, there are so many places that Francine has never seen. I'd like to show them to her. We'll see you again as soon as her folks find a suitable place to live."

Just as Ray finished his sentence, Francine came down the stairs and greeted her husband with a warm kiss. "Looks like you got here earlier than you planned," she said. "I'm packed and ready to go so we can leave anytime you want."

"OK honey," Ray said, "seems like now is as good a time as any, so let's hit the road."

With their good-byes said all around, Ray picked up Francine's suitcase, and they headed for the car. They were soon on the turnpike headed west, and Francine was snuggled up to him with her hand resting on his leg.

"Do you know how much I love you?" she said, as she kissed his neck.

"What about your first husband?" Ray asked. "Did you love him as much as me? After all, I was hoping for a little fooling around tonight!"

Francine played along with the game and said, "Well, since he left me alone for so long, I was hoping you might." They teased for awhile and then settled into some more serious conversation when she asked, "What are the plans now?"

"First stop is to the license bureau for a new marriage license, and then we'll get married again with the Gulardi name. Then we'll check in with your mom and dad and decide our next move together. Honey, we can go anywhere in the country or anywhere in the world, for that matter, and stay as long as we want. We are rich beyond your wildest dreams, which even shocks me! Before we went back east, we had plenty, but now we have twice as much. We're the new owners of three houses, one plant, and our own Enterprise Company. I have retained the lawyer you recommended overseeing our interests there. The property alone is worth another fortune. I haven't even counted the bank account left to me. I thought that perhaps you might like to take a real honeymoon cruise for a couple weeks to an island someplace. I'd like my new wife to have the kind of honeymoon she'll never forget!"

Teasing him she said, "OK, I guess that sounds like a good idea so I'll just go along for the ride."

Ray put his arm around her, gave her a hug and said, "So be it, this time next week, we'll be on a cruise ship headed for the Virgin Islands. Why don't you call your folks tonight and let them know we're getting married again, and we'll be honeymooning overseas. When we come back, we'll go see them. You can introduce them to your newest new husband."

"You sure are enjoying this second marriage thing," she said. "With this getting married, getting the marriage annulled, and getting married again."

"I'm sorry honey," Ray said, "its just that I'm so happy to know my true heritage and my true history. I promise I won't say any more about it, at least for awhile."

Ray was true to his word and didn't discuss the issue through their second marriage or through their honeymoon cruise.

All too soon two beautiful weeks had passed. It was all Ray and his bride had hoped for and would always remember. They arrived back in Las Vegas and picked up their car from long-term parking and decided to drive to Kingman, Arizona and stay there for the night. Ray said, "We can get up early in the morning and drive to Phoenix and meet with your folks."

"I'd like that," Francine said, "and maybe they've found a place to live there. One thing's for sure, it's warm there. Dad didn't want to be shoveling snow anymore".

"Well, that's the good thing about that area. They don't have to live in snow country, but if they wanted to see some now and then, all they have to do is drive to Flagstaff and see all the snow they want."

Around noon the next day, they arrived at the motel in Phoenix where Francine's parents were staying. They lovingly greeted each other and talked for awhile. Ray could appreciate the fact that Francine and her folks might like some time together alone so he told them he wanted to get the car serviced and left. He found a Jiffy Lube reasonably close to the motel and after telling the people there what servicing he wanted done and with some time to kill, he decided to take a walk and call his contact in Virginia.

"Thought I'd better check in," Ray said, "We just got back yesterday from our honeymoon and drove to Phoenix to see her folks."

The contact said, "How about your name change, did you get it done?"

"Yes, that's all taken care of, and then we drove to Vegas and got married again with my real name."

"Congratulations Ray," his contact said, "but until we get you signed up again with your new name, don't get in any trouble that we can't get you out of."

"No sweat there," Ray said, "taking a leave is what I wanted to do so we can travel for awhile. There are so many places my wife hasn't seen. I'm anxious to show them all to her. When we were in the Virgin Islands, she was like a kid with a new toy. I wonder what it will be like for her in Europe and the Far East. China is like no other place on earth. Then, it's on around the globe. Maybe she'll fall in love with someplace, and we'll stay there for awhile."

"That sound like a good plan, Ray. So far no one has made a move back east to take over."

"Do you remember I told you about Ken Walls, AKA Shooter?" Ray asked. "Well, before I left back there, I made him the boss in my place and any changes regarding a takeover or anything else, I'll be informed immediately. I'll give you a call. Additionally, if you hear anything I should be aware of, you call me." They hung up and the next call was to Shooter.

Shooter answered and said, "Well hello boss. I wondered when you were going to call. How is your trip so far?"

"Nothing could be better Shooter," Ray said. "We honeymooned in the Islands, and we're leaving for a world tour very soon— but I'll still call you once a week. How are things back there? Anybody else come in yet?"

"Not yet," Shooter said, "We see a couple new faces every now and then. Rocko did say that one guy looked familiar, but he couldn't remember where he's seen him. The house is starting to look good. They're laying the foundations now, and the basement is finished. He hopes to have it under roof in three weeks. Everything else is looking good.

"Hope you don't mind, but Rocko is staying loose and away in case someone wants to hire him. If that were to happen, we'd have an inside man that we could trust."

"I don't mind in the least," Ray said. "Sounds like you boys have it all under control. I can enjoy my trip knowing I've left the business in capable hands. Don't forget the lawyer if you ever need him. I'll call again next week, but in the meantime, don't work too hard. Talk to you soon."

Ray paid for the servicing on his car and drove back to the motel to meet with Francine and her folks. That night at dinner he outlined their plans to her mom and dad.

"We don't know how long we'll travel, but when Francine has had enough, we'll look for a place. By that time, maybe you'll have found a place too. Any ideas yet where you might like to land?"

"Not really," Francine's father said, "So far we've considered three states. We were going to head back to Lower California and then make our decision. Mom heard so much about the weather there so that might be our final choice."

"Weather wise, I'd have to agree with her," Ray said, "but tax wise, I'd have to pick someplace else."

"They're still having trouble back home," Francine said, "and I wish they could stop all the drugs and maybe the killing would stop too. The day we left, there was a big explosion in front of Tony's Restaurant, and they said on the news that some people were killed."

Francine's dad added, "Yeah, Mom called Carol and Bob, and they said that three died immediately, and the other one died the next day. According to Bob, it looked like a gang hit. Ray, will this have any affect on what you have back there?"

"Not a bit," Ray said, "All of our business is honest and above board. I agree that the killing should stop, but I also hate to see so many people hurt by the slow death caused by dope. But, on a lighter note, when are you and mom leaving?"

"Well," dad said, "the only thing that was holding us here at all was you and Francine, so I guess we could leave tomorrow."

"We're going to put my car in storage here so tomorrow I'll find a reputable facility for it," Ray said, "and then we'll start our trip from here. Fly to Frisco as soon as we're ready. From that point on, the world is available for wherever we want to go. When Francine gets tired of traveling, we'll settle down someplace. Who knows, it might be in an area close to you folks. When we return from all this traveling, I'll have to go back to Camden and make sure everything is moving along according to plan. I'm hoping that by that time you'll be settled, Francine can stay with you so the girls can catch up on all the places they've been and things they've seen."

When they had finished dinner, Ray paid the bill, and he and Francine told her parent's goodnight.

"See you in the morning for breakfast."

"Make it around six," her father said, "we want to be on the road before it gets too hot."

Once they were alone, Ray said, "Honey, when your parents

leave in the morning, I have some last minute errands to run so I hope you won't mind waiting for me in our room. I'll be back to pick you up as soon as possible." Francine agreed, and they spent much of their night making love.

The following morning, after breakfast they watched as her parents drove away for their own trip and search for a new home. Francine said, "I know you have to leave now, but I'll be ready when you get back; and if there's any change of plans, will you call me?"

"Darling, you know I'll call you if anything changes," Ray said. "In fact, I might just call you even if there aren't any changes, just to hear your voice, but at any rate, I should be back in a couple hours. Once I take care of these few things, I'll have to put the car in storage so look for me in a taxi."

When Ray left, he had a desire to wet his whistle so he stopped at a convenience store and purchased a quart of beer which the cashier put in a paper sack. It always amused him that you can't walk out of a store showing a can of beer or bottle of booze but the very shape the sack takes tells the world what you've purchased. From the store, he drove to a wayside park and removed the bonds from under the back seat. He put the other remote and composite C explosive under the seat and drove to a UPS store where he got two mailing envelopes. He split the bonds, putting half into one envelope and half into the other. He asked to borrow a phone book and got the addresses of a local Salvation Army and Hospice and mailed an envelope of bonds to each. Once that was done, he checked addresses for vehicle storage locations and drove to one that was fairly close.

Ray liked the layout of the storage facility and rented a garage for two months, just in case. Once he had backed his car in, the manager unhooked the battery and asked Ray to lock the car, which he did. The manager asked Ray if he'd like insurance on the contents of the car.

"No," Ray said, "there's nothing that can be stolen except the car itself. In fact, I have an extra key, so why don't you take the spare in case it has to be moved."

The manager said, "No, that's not necessary as we have camera's set up and the whole building is concrete. Some people buy the insurance to make themselves feel better. No one has ever lost anything, but it is a good moneymaker."

"Yes," Ray said, "I can see where it would be. Any possibility that you could call me a cab?"

"You got it," the manager said, "Come on down to the office and I'll take care of it."

Chapter 39

Ray got lucky, and the taxi arrived within fifteen minutes. He was soon on his way back to the motel. When he entered the motel room, Francine was all packed and looking quite beautiful. She was wearing a baby pink dress that was almost off the shoulder with ruffles trimmed in white. The skirt of the dress was made up of ruffle after ruffle, with each one getting wider as it got closer to the hem. Her pink shoes matched her dress, and a pink ribbon pulled her beautiful dark hair away from her face.

"Damn you look good," Ray said, "Maybe we should stay awhile longer!"

Francine laughed and teasingly said, "No my love, you'll just have to wait until tonight when we get settled, that's if you play your cards right."

"OK honey, have it your way, but you'll have to decide before we leave Frisco where you want to go. There are a lot of places to choose like the Islands, Far East or even France. What's your choice?"

"I think I'd like to start with Japan. I've heard it is quite beautiful. From there, we can go anywhere you want. I'd like to see it all."

Ray called a cab and after waiting a few minutes, picked up their luggage, and they headed for the front door of the motel.

Francine was only a few steps ahead of Ray. As she walked out the door, shots came from the street. A motorcycle with two people on it and a car were exchanging gunfire. When the driver of the car was hit, the car crashed as the motorcycle took off. Everything had happened so fast. Ray had seen Francine go down and thought she had ducked as the shots rang out. But now, as he went to her to help her up, he saw the red stain seeping on the pink ruffle between her breasts and knew that she had taken a direct hit to the heart. His Francine was dead.

He sat down on the sidewalk and gently held her in his arms, rocking back and forth, crying softly. She was still warm, she still looked beautiful, and although he knew she was gone, he couldn't believe it. The pain in his own heart felt like it was he who had taken the deadly shot.

Someone had called the police and an ambulance. Ray could hear the sirens somewhere in the back of his head, but for the moment, nothing was making sense to him. When the ambulance arrived, they checked Francine for signs of life...there were none.

The police had put up yellow tape around the scene, and people were gathering. The police were taking pictures of Francine, but Ray saw nothing except the love of his life lying in his arms. The attendants from the ambulance told him they'd have to take her now, but he held on to her as though by holding her, he could bring her back. They had to literally pry her from his arms. This man who so seldom showed emotion was quietly sobbing as the doors to the ambulance closed with his Francine inside.

Ray's head was spinning, and the ache in his heart made it almost impossible to breathe but he had to think. "I've got to think. I've got to figure this out." Ray was talking out loud and finally the old Ray kicked in. He realized there were things that had to be done, and only he could do them.

He reached for his cell phone and called Francine's parents.

"Mom, it's me, Ray," he said. "I need you to come back to the motel; there's been a bad accident here!"

Her mother said, "Ray, it has to be Francine. What happened?"

"There were some people involved in a drive-by shooting just as we stepped out of the motel door, and she was shot," Ray said.

Francine's mother was crying but said, "Dad is turning around now, and we'll be there as soon as we can."

As Ray hung up, the ambulance driver asked him where he'd like the body to go.

"I don't know," Ray said. "We're not from around here so could you recommend a good funeral home?"

The driver said, "Hendricks is a good one. I'd recommend them, and they're only a couple blocks from here".

Using his cell phone, Ray asked to be connected to the Hendricks

Funeral Home. Once the phone was answered, he asked to speak to the director. When the phone was again answered, the voice said, "This is Keith, how may I help you?"

"My name is Raymond Gulardi, and my wife has just been killed," Ray said. "They're holding her body in an ambulance as we speak. I'd like them to take her to your funeral home now. I'll be there tomorrow to make the final arrangements if that's alright."

"Mr. Gulardi, I am so sorry for your loss," the funeral director said. "Yes, please have them bring her here now. I'll be expecting you tomorrow. Just ask for Keith."

Ray thanked him and gave the ambulance driver instructions to take Francine directly to the funeral home. He watched the ambulance carrying his wife until it was out of sight. When he turned around, a police detective was waiting to talk to him.

"I realize this is a bad time for you sir, but we could use your help," the detective said. "What did you see that might help us solve this crime?"

"There were two men on the motorcycle, and the one on the back was exchanging gunfire with the car that crashed. then the motorcycle took off down the road."

"Was there anything about the bike, driver, or passenger that stood out?" the detective asked.

"Not much except that the driver was wearing a jacket with some kind of emblem on the back, but I couldn't make out what the emblem was, or even the color. Everything happened so fast," Ray said.

"I can understand that," the detective said. "Well, the driver of the car is dead, and the other guy swears he was only a passenger, but at any rate, he's going to jail."

"Is he from around here or this area?" Ray asked.

"Yes," the detective said. "His name is Ben Meanes. He's been in trouble before. Belongs to the Marauders, a local Chino gang. Just a guess on my part, but I'd bet money those two on the bike were outlaws."

"Detective, if you need me, I'll be here at the motel. My wife's parents left this morning, but I called them and they're on their way back."

The detective left, and Ray took the suitcases back into the motel. He asked the desk clerk if he could get his room back but was told the maids were cleaning it so she gave him a key card to a new room. Ray thanked her and took the bags to the room he'd been assigned.

Once he was inside the room, the silence was deafening. He just couldn't believe what had transpired since he and Francine had left their room only a short time ago. Because Ray had never been much of an emotional man, the pain in his chest from the heartache was foreign and somewhat confusing to him. He realized he had never loved anyone with such depth as he had, and still did, love Francine. He didn't want to believe she was gone.

"Snap out of it!" he said to himself and left the room to await Francine's parents.

The thirty-minute wait seemed like a lifetime, but finally they pulled into the driveway. Ray went out to meet them. It was only when Francine's mom got out of the car and saw Ray standing there alone, did the full impact of the situation really hit her.

All she said was, "Oh my God, Francine is gone."

Ray caught her just as her legs gave way. He picked her up and carried her to the lobby.

The desk clerk saw what happened and quickly brought a glass of water and cold cloth for Francine's mom. When she came around, Ray told them the whole story, and the fact that he had allowed the ambulance to take Francine's body to the funeral home. He was supposed to go there tomorrow to make arrangements.

"I'd like you to go with me if you want to because she was your daughter and you have the right to make arrangements as much as I do. I also have her suitcase in my room, and you can have that. I only ask that I have a few pictures from our honeymoon that she had in there."

Her mom hesitated a moment and said, "Ray, you can have whatever you want, but isn't it ironic that the whole life of your child can fit into one small suitcase?" With that, Francine's mother once again started to sob and was comforted by her husband who also had tears flowing down his cheeks.

Ray said, "When you both want to leave in the morning, I'll be ready, but tonight I need to be alone. I hope you don't mind."

Ray left the motel and spotted a bar across the road and decided to have a few drinks, hoping it would take his mind off what had happened. When he went in, he noticed that the place was fairly dark and almost empty except for a few people in booths near the back. He sat at the bar and was the only patron there.

He really didn't want to talk so he ordered first one good stiff drink,which went down in one swallow, and then another. He sat there with his head bowed, and a million things went through his mind. "God, why did you take my Francine away?" He felt he was being punished and thought that perhaps it was because of the kind of work that he did.

After all, and in reality, he was an assassin, a paid killer. He was paid for death. But as that thought came to his mind, he shook it off because he didn't kill for the sake of killing; he killed the ones that made other people's lives miserable with their dope and guns and forced prostitution.

Because the bartender had no one else to talk to, he decided to strike up a conversation with Ray and said, "Man, did you hear what happened at the motel across the street? Those damn gang-bangers. One of these days, someone it going to get real mad and do something about it 'cause it's damn sure the police can't because the judge turns them loose. They can't get the right evidence because no one ever sees anything. They see alright. They're just too damn scared to speak up. Someday I hope the vigilantes come back and clean up this town."

"Tell me, did you see what happened from here?"

"When the shooting started," the bartender said, "I looked out that window about the time the car crashed, and the motorcycle took off towards town. They have a club about two miles out on Highway #10."

"How do you know where they went?" Ray asked.

The bartender said, "Just a guess by the clothes they had on."

"What about the guys in the car? Someone said a Chino gang. They bad?"

"Yes," the bartender said, "As bad as the outlaws. Both want the dope trade, and they fight all the time."

Ray was slightly inebriated from the heavy booze he wasn't used to and the whole thing really pissed him off, and he said, "It's a damn shame there aren't any men in this town with enough backbone to end all this shit!"

"Don't sell us short," the bartender said, "There are a couple ex-rangers who come in here that nobody screws with. I believe they could be bad and have no regrets if someone messed with them. If you're in town tomorrow night, they're usually here around six thirty. They're both guards at Brinks."

"Do these guys talk about getting even if someone did screw with them?" Ray asked.

The bartender said, "No, they hardly talk at all. It's just the way they look and act that makes you just know. And anyway the big talkers are usually all air; it's the quiet one's you have to look out for."

"Yeah, I guess that's true," Ray said. "Give me a six pack to go, and I might see you tomorrow night, 'cause who knows what fate has in store."

Chapter 40

Ray returned to his room, opened a beer, and turned on the TV to watch the news. Later in the newscast, they talked about a gang-related shooting that left two people dead. Not once did they mention that one of the dead was an innocent bystander, his wife.

Seeing it on the news made Ray angrier than he was already. His mind was hard at work thinking about how to make them pay for what he'd lost. Funny how a few drinks can relax the mind, and sometimes clear the brain. He was the expert, he knew all the tricks of the trade, but all his thinking revolved around his sniper rifle—but then a real plan started to form. Taking the extra effort would have to wait until the funeral was over, but then, without his Francine, he had nothing but time on his hands—and nowhere to go.

Ray turned off the TV, took a very hot shower, and went to bed. Sleep eluded him for hours because he kept remembering Francine in her pink dress with the red seeping through the ruffles. What rest he got was only fitful dozing so he finally got up around seven to meet her parents for breakfast in the restaurant. When he arrived, they were already there.

Ray was solemn as he bid her parents good morning, although they all knew the morning wasn't good at all. He said, "Were you folks able to get any rest?"

"Not much rest and no sleep," her mother said. "We talked about what Francine would have wanted and because we had discussed cremation for ourselves, Francine had said she would want to be cremated as well. Would you agree to do what she wanted Ray?"

Although his own heart was breaking, it went out to Francine's parents because their pain and loss was so evident so he said, "How could I want anything different? She was yours so many years and mine so short a time. What about the funeral? Are there any special things we need?"

"We don't believe in funerals, and neither did Francine," her mom said. "We believe that when we die, people should remember us as we were when alive, not the last time when they saw us dead. Her ashes should be sprinkled in Camden Cemetery, as ours will be one day. She was born there in that town so now she will return. Carol and Bob will be there to say their good-byes."

"When her ashes are ready," Ray said, "I'll buy the tickets for the three of us so we can fly back to Camden together and then return here. Since you've told me what her wishes were, you can both stay here while I make all the arrangements if you want."

"Oh, if you would do that, we'd so much appreciate it," her mother said. "If we went down there, we'd just have to see her. This way we can remember the last time we saw her and said goodbye to her this morning."

Ray said he would take care of everything and left the restaurant. He went straight to the front desk and asked the desk clerk to call him a taxi. Ray didn't have to wait long, and his first stop was to the storage facility to retrieve his car.

Back in the driver's seat, he drove to Hendricks Funeral Home to make the final arrangements for Francine. Keith, the funeral director, assured him that everything would be taken care of, and Francine's remains would be ready to be picked up in two days.

Once the arrangements had been made, Keith handed Ray the jewelry that Francine had been wearing. He looked at her watch, her earrings, and her wedding ring. It was difficult to hold back the tears that suddenly stung his eyes.

Keith's next question brought Ray back to reality when he asked, "How would you like her obituary to read?"

"Only her name and the fact that she was a victim of foul play, no other details. The notice will run in her hometown where she was raised and where her relatives are. If that's all you need me for, I'll be back around seven, two days from now to pick up her ashes."

Ray called Francine's parents and asked them to meet him in the motel restaurant around lunchtime. He arrived first and ordered coffee for all of them. As the coffee was brought to the table, her parents walked in. They all ordered a light lunch, and while waiting for the food, Ray said, "Mom and Dad, I've done a lot of soul searching to arrive at what I'm going to say.

"In my heart, I've already told Francine goodbye, so I think it would be best if the two of you flew back to Camden alone. You can stay at Carol and Bob's by yourselves. I'll take you to the airport here when you leave. I'll pick you up at the airport when you come back. Your tickets will be at the airport here, and a car will be waiting for you when you get there—or I'll have my manager pick you up. Whatever you want or need, just let Shooter know, and he'll take care of everything.

"Francine's ashes will be ready day after tomorrow so now it's up to you to decide on the actual plan."

Mom said, "It sounds like you have everything taken care of. What do you think Dad?"

"Ray I understand how you feel," Dad said. "Francine is gone now, but I want you to know that we accepted you in our lives as she did. You will always be our son and part of our family. We'll do as you've suggested and take Francine home. We should be back in a couple days."

As they walked out of the restaurant, Ray told them that he was going to see the police detective who was handling the case.

"Maybe he's found out something," Ray said, "so I'll see you both later."

Ray's first stop was to the airport where he purchased the tickets and made arrangements for a car. The flight would depart at nine twenty in the morning three days from now. He decided to wait until later this evening to call Shooter to tell him everything that had happened.

With everything taken care of for Francine's parents, he drove to the police station and asked the desk sergeant if Detective Steve Mann was available. The desk sergeant used the intercom to inform Mann that someone wanted to see him.

"Who is he and what does he want?" The voice could be heard saying.

Ray said, "It's Ray Gulardi from the Howard Johnson's, and it was my wife that was shot there."

"Please come back to my office and I'll meet you at the door," was the response coming from the speaker.

As the sergeant flipped off the intercom switch, he pointed down the hall and told Ray it was the door on the left. By the time he got there, Detective Steve Mann was already opening the door, invited him in, and offered him a seat.

"I was coming out to see you today but you've saved me a trip. How can I help you?"

"I was hoping the boy you have in custody might know something," Ray said.

"This is the part of my job I hate," Steve said. "According to him, he was only a passenger and had caught a ride when the shooting started. He did say he fired back in self-defense so it looks like he might walk because they'll say he's only a child. Child, my ass, nineteen years old is no child!"

How about the other guy?" Ray asked.

"Both of them have a long rap sheet, B&E, assault and stolen cars, most before they were eighteen, so the ridiculous part is the fact that those records were sealed by the Court. Oh yeah, the other guy was twenty-four and also a member of the Chino Marauders. Believe me, I'm sorry I can't give you any good news. I wish we could have gotten the other two; and there again, from what I understand, they too are gang members."

"Detective," Ray said, "Thank you for your help. I realize your hands are tied so I'll say goodbye for now. Please let me know if you hear anything."

Chapter 41

When Ray left the police station, he drove west on Highway #10; about three miles out of town, he spotted a house which sat back off the highway almost to the woods behind the place. In front were a couple dozen motor cycles so this had to be their clubhouse. Ray checked out the place very carefully and saw there were numerous possibilities here as there was nothing close on either side.

He turned around and headed back through town almost due east. He had driven only a couple more miles when he passed what looked like another clubhouse, considering all the cars parked in front. Here again, the place was set back by itself, but the house on one side was set closer to the road and trees separated the two houses. Ray made a mental note of the layout of both places and headed to the little bar he had been in the night before.

The same bartender was on duty and he said, "Good afternoon sir, what can I get you?"

Ray was sitting in the same spot as the night before and ordered a mixed drink to help pass a little time. When the bartender brought Ray his drink, he said, "Would you care for anything else?"

"No, not right now," Ray said. "Maybe a sandwich a little later. I just wanted to unwind a little before I go back to the motel."

The place was virtually empty at that time of the day so the bartender was grateful for the possibility of conversation and asked, "Do you work in town or on vacation?"

Ray said, "Just passing through, but think I'll stick around a few days. This place looks interesting and who know what might turn up."

"I wish you luck," the bartender said, "It gets mighty hot in the summer, but the rest of the time is real nice. If you decide to buy a place, just check out the area real good before you plunk down any money."

Ray's eyebrows raised and with a quizzical look he said, "Oh, you mean there are some bad places around here?"

The bartender said, "Yes, especially right now. They've got a war going on, and although it's not real big yet, you saw what happened here the other day."

"You're talking about a gang war?" Ray asked.

"You know it!" the bartender said. "Both sides want more territory, and both sides are nothing but thugs and killers."

"How do you tell them apart?" Ray asked. "It seems like the motorcycle gang wears colors, but how about the others?

The bartender said, "Normally, most wear blue scarves around their heads or necks, but when there's trouble, they change the color to red, like the Bloods".

"Thanks," Ray said, "I'll keep that in mind. I guess I'll call it a night. Maybe I'll see you tomorrow."

The next day and night went by with no new developments. On the following morning, and with great sadness, Ray drove Francine's parents to the funeral home to claim her ashes. From there, he drove them to the airport and asked them to call him with their schedule so he could pick them up on their return trip. At the departure gate, Mom kissed him on the cheek before they left.

As he was driving out of the airport, a sudden thought came to Ray. Now he knew how to get even for the loss of his Francine. Tonight he planned to watch the Chino's Clubhouse to see when the activity slowed way down because he had a present he wanted to deliver.

His first stop was to a clothing store where he purchased a dark set of coveralls, along with a red scarf and headband.

With time on his hands, he drove by the gang's clubhouse once more while it was light enough to see where he would later leave his car and checkout what would be the best approach to the house. Now he was ready for tonight. From there, he found a place to eat, then went back to his room to watch TV and wait.

When two a.m. rolled around, Ray put on the dark coveralls and left his room to deliver his present. Before hitting the road, he removed the last remote package from under his seat, and now he was ready to let them enjoy it.

Ray parked at the location he had previously selected and carried the package toward the house. As he approached, he noticed there were only a couple cars in front, and there wasn't any noise coming from the house. No lights could be seen.

The closer he got, the more he realized how small this place was, probably no more than a one bedroom. He approached the back of the house and opened the door for the crawl space. He quietly went underneath the house and placed the package close to the center of the house and on top of the foundation. Ray had been trained well, and his activity was silent. He left as quietly as he had entered, reached his car, and drove home. When he got back to his room, he took a hot shower before going to bed and slept late the next day.

While at breakfast the next morning, his cell phone rang. It was Francine's mom.

"Hello mom," Ray said. "How are you doing?"

"We're holding up," was her response. "We've been to the cemetery and wanted to let you know that our plane will be arriving tomorrow at 11:10 a.m."

"OK Mom," Ray said. "I'll pick you up at the baggage claim. See you then, and please tell Carol and Bob hello for me. Don't worry mom; I'll be there to get you."

When he had finished breakfast, Ray approached the desk clerk at the motel and paid for two rooms for two more nights. He then drove by the Outlaw's place one more time. Everything was set in his mind...he was ready. From there he drove to the bar because he suddenly wanted some company.

When the bartender saw Ray, he said, "Well hello again, glad you stopped by. This place has been pretty dead today so I could use some good conversation."

"Me too," Ray said. "And I need a good cold beer and soft seat as well."

"How's the search coming along?" the bartender asked.

"Not too good," Ray said. "I may try Tucson and see what might be available there…but I might stay a couple more days to check out the job market."

"Well, I hope you find what you're looking for; wherever that might be."

Knowing full well that he'd be leaving here for good, Ray said. "Thank you. You never know what might happen or what might come along; we'll just have to wait and see."

The next day Ray picked up Francine's parents at the airport, and on the way back to the motel, they told him how they had spread her ashes at the cemetery. There was so much sadness in Ray's heart, but he told them he'd be leaving to return to the business in Camden.

"With Francine gone, I have no desire to travel anymore so I might as well stay busy."

"We'll be going tomorrow as well. So how about joining us for breakfast?" Mom asked.

"Glad to Mom," Ray said. "Remember my new name is Gulardi, and you can call me anytime to fill me in on your travels, and let me know where you are."

Almost before Ray knew it, they were eating breakfast for what could be their last time together. Although no words were spoken about it, the empty place at the table loomed at them like a menacing shadow. She had been greatly loved and was now sadly missed.

Ray watched them drive away on their way to California. He knew his time here was short. He returned to his room and saw Francine's forgotten suitcase there. He sadly went through her things and once he was confidant that it contained only clothes, put both her suitcase and his in the car. Ray asked for directions to the women's shelter and drove there to donate the suitcase containing her clothes. Perhaps this small token of Francine's generous heart would help someone in need.

Ray found a park and selected a location away from other cars, raised the back seat, and removed the sniper rifle with suppressor. He removed the extra long clip to confirm in his mind that it was fully loaded and placed it back into the weapon, which he then placed on the floor within his reach. He took out the red band, placed it on the ground, and walked on it a few times to give the appearance that it had been worn. Now he was ready.

Suddenly he realized that he had forgotten the most important detail. How stupid could he be? Fingerprints were a no no! Ray drove to a drugstore, bought a pair of rubber gloves, and a box of tissues, and returned to the park. He removed the clip and took out all the bullets, put on the rubber gloves, wiped each bullet completely, and replaced them in the clip. He then cleaned the clip thoroughly, wiped down the rifle, replaced the clip, and laid the rifle back down on the floor. He took off the rubber gloves and put them on the seat beside him. Now he was sure he was ready. When he left the park, he drove past the Chino Marauder's hangout and stopped at a truck stop on Highway #10. He gassed up his car and went in for a meal.

Ray ate slowly because there was plenty of time, too much time in fact, and he was deep in thought. Waiting was the hardest part of any job, but it did allow him time to plan his next move. He had been thinking about this a lot at night while lying in bed alone.

Francine had been his life and losing her made him bitter. He wanted revenge, and tonight without remorse, he would have it. He would make toothpicks out of the Chino clubhouse and hopefully take out a fair number of the gang as well.

Once it started to get dark, Ray got into his car and removed the remote from the glove compartment. He took his time on the drive back toward town. When he was fairly close to the clubhouse, he stopped the car and put the rubber gloves back on. He drove slowly, saw a few cars parked in front, and gave the remote a kiss before flipping the switch that set it off. It was instantly speeding down the road toward the Outlaw's clubhouse.

He parked on the road and fired non-stop, shredding the building; then worked on the motorcycles, causing some of them to explode and making others totally unusable. He threw the red headband down and thought that with some luck, the Marauders would be blamed for this damage.

With his job finished here, he took off toward Tucson, Arizona, on his way back to Virginia for his next assignment. He didn't look back as he pondered his future, but the one thing he was sure of, his Francine had been avenged.

The Sequel

Paid For Death ~The Return~

ISBN: 978-0-9845904-7-6

Rice Brothers Mysteries by Niles Rader

Death Was Inevitable
ISBN: 978-0-9768677-4-6

Betrayed by Greed
SBN: 978-0-9778311-3-5

Death Does Not Wait
ISBN: 978-0-9845904-2-1

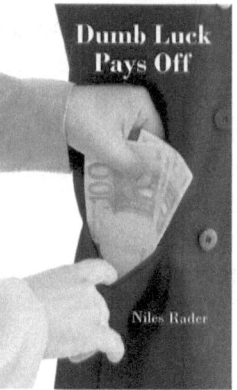

Dumb Luck Pays Off
ISBN: 978-0-9768677-2-2

The Root of Evil
ISBN: 978-0-9768677-5-3

Death by Deceit
ISBN: 978-0-9823703-4-6

Other Mysteries by Niles Rader

Paid For Death
ISBN: 978-0-9710954-8-9

Paid For Death ~The Return~
ISBN: 978-0-9845904-7-6

A Sister's Revenge
ISBN: 978-0-9778311-6-6

Lie To Love
ISBN: 978-0-9778311-4-2

Retribution
ISBN: 978-0-9778311-2-8

Live Smart or Die Dumb
ISBN: 978-0-9710954-4-1

www.ingramcontent.com/pod-product-compliance
Lightning Source LLC
Chambersburg PA
CBHW020648260626
47157CB00008B/2956